THE TRACES OF MERRILEE

THE TRACES OF MERRILEE

HERBERT BREAN

WILDSIDE PRESS

For Lyd Morrison, with love.

Published by Wildside Press LLC.
www.wildsidebooks.com

PROLOGUE

I guess you could say it began this way, but it's a hell of a prosaic beginning.

We were having dinner at Twit-Twit's.

There had been smoked salmon, soft as butter and sprinkled with capers and finely chopped onion. Then stuffed chicken breasts, the stuffing touched with dill and fresh parsley. Pouilly Fumé with that, in well-chilled glasses. Endive salad, and then a kind of tangy Scandinavian cheese that I can't remember the name of, but Twit-Twit likes, and that tastes wonderful with crusty French bread. Then espresso and Armagnac.

The four of us were out on Twit-Twit's terrace. It was April, and the New York night was warm and soft and lovely. And you thought of Paris.

Naturally.

Twit-Twit looked fantastically, inhumanly beautiful. In her vixenish way.

Tom Dolan said, "God damn everything."

His wife Betsy, who has blue eyes if ever there were blue eyes, said, "Here we go again," and splashed a little Armagnac in everyone's glass.

I was holding Twit-Twit's hand and looking up at the night sky. There was no moon, and thank heaven for that; it would have been too theatrical. But you could see stars. I thought how nice it was to have everything go right occasionally and the dice throw a seven at the right time, by themselves.

I sipped the brandy, chuckled at Tom's remark, and said, "Of course. Nuts to the universe."

But Tom can be moody. He's Irish, of course. Who isn't?

He said, "I mean it. Betsy and I are all loused up."

That's the kind of remark that could disturb you, coming from most people when they have had a couple of drinks. Not the Dolans. They seem to fight all the time, they really never do, and they're awfully nice. Also, they are deeply in love. After many years.

I said, "Now what? But why don't you tell us about it somewhere else? We've had a wonderful dinner. So let Twit-Twit and I take you out. Like to the belly dancers."

"Which belly dancers?"

"Any belly dancers. Any anything. There are the joints at Twenty-eighth Street. There are other joints nearby, in midtown."

"No," Tom said. "I'm serious. For a moment."

Suddenly I knew he was. Tom is a tall, serious-looking guy who is seldom serious. So when he is, it is really impressive.

He said, "I had lunch today with a man who made me think."

"Beginner's luck," said Betsy. But she looked at him appraisingly. We all know Tom.

"We got talking," Tom said. "And after a while this guy raised an interesting question. He said to me, 'If you had only one day left to live, but you could arrange it so that you could spend the day doing anything you wanted—anything—what would you choose to do? How would you arrange that day?'"

"Well, how would you?" I said.

Tom looked up at the darkly glowing Manhattan sky. "You could do or have anything you want. Anything. Your last day on earth." He fell silent.

"I can tell you how I'd spend it," said Twit-Twit. "Paris. I'd spend the morning at Dior, buying clothes. And I'd spend the afternoon wearing them."

"And the evening?" Betsy said.

"Cocktails at the Ritz bar. Dinner at Lapérouse, at one of the tables on the second floor, overlooking the river. Then a walk up the river to see Notre Dame lighted at night."

Tom was studying her. "And then?"

"Then—I don't know." She looked at me and blushed a little, which is a lot for Twit-Twit, because she doesn't blush easily, and it was nice to notice that she had looked at me before she did.

"So your choice would be Paris," said Betsy. "What's yours, Deac?" She was still worried about Tom.

"It's an interesting idea. It tells you something about yourself, doesn't it? Like a Rorschach test. I'd spend the day working on a story I liked a lot, preferably a murder. Then I'd pick up Twit-Twit and take her for a little stroll around the Place Vendôme to the Ritz bar and buy her all the Martinis she wanted. Then the Left Bank, as she said. Then—"

Betsy laughed; she has a nice laugh. "Okay, your choice would be just to be with Twit-Twit. Tom?"

"God damn it," said Tom. "But I said that before."

"You certainly did," his wife told him.

"Here's what's bugging me," and I knew that whatever was coming, he would mean it. "Today we filmed the last show for the season. I'm free until August—no more TV shows, stars, cameramen, or anything to worry about. So suddenly Bets and I decided we'd blow ourselves to a little holiday. France. Paris. Le Cote d'Or. And we would sail on the Montmartre. So we call up and discover we can't get on the Montmartre. She's booked solid for *the sailing the day after tomorrow, and she's also booked solid for the next sailing, two weeks from now."*

His fingers rapped the table.

"That's why I got going on how to spend a day perfectly. Suddenly Bets and I want to have a nice relaxing trip on a nice ship. That would be my idea of how to spend your last day perfectly. We have the time and for once we have the money, which is always a sometime thing. But we can't get on the only ship we really want at the moment. So God damn it. What else can I say?"

"That's a shame," said Twit-Twit. "I know how you feel. Because I'm free for the next two weeks, and I was thinking only this morning of a fast trip to Paris. I was dreaming of a plane. But the Montmartre *would be even better."*

I began to consider something. I suppose what Tom had said about spending the last day of your life happily had a little to do with it, even though I'm not exactly at the three-score-and-ten stage. I'm only about halfway there, as a matter of fact. Nevertheless—

Twit-Twit said, "Betsy, how about you? What would your perfect day be like?"

Betsy took a cigarette, accepted Tom's light, inhaled deeply, and leaned back.

"Let me see," she said thoughtfully. "I've never planned this kind of thing before. But I'd wake up about ten in the morning and have breakfast in bed. The breakfast would be brought to me by Cary Grant. In slacks and baby-blue sports jacket. Then, after a tub and clothes, I'd go out in my Rolls—"

"Driven by Gregory Peck," said Tom.

"And Richard Burton. One would drive and one would be footman. I don't care which is which. I'd drive to Harry Winston's and shop for diamonds. Then—"

Betsy went on. But I didn't listen, amusing as it was.

Like Tom, I'd, had lunch that day with a guy, and he had said some things that had made me think, too. Quite different kinds of things. And sometimes you go a little nutty.

Maybe it was just the Armagnac. Anyway, I got quietly up and went to the phone, which is in the bedroom, well out of earshot. I called the guy I'd had lunch with. We spoke a few minutes.

I came back.

"...night flight to Copenhagen," Betsy was saying. "I might be a little tired at this point, so they would have put a tub aboard the plane for me. Filled with perfume, of course. No water. Then I'd read a first folio of Hamlet *while my maid spoon-fed me a little caviar. And just outside, a string quartet would be playing..."*

I sat down and found Twit-Twit's hand.

"Do you really want to go to Paris'?" I asked her.

"Do you know anyone who doesn't want to go to Paris?"

"I said 'really.'" Her eyes gave me one of their blue-green looks.

"What the hell do you mean really? You stumble-tongued Irish bum?"

"Because if you want, I think we're all going. In a good suite in the Montmartre. All together. You and I and the Dolans here. They'll chaperone us, of course. Everything will be very proper."

"You had too many Negronis before dinner." But Tom knew I meant it. We understand each other.

"I always have too many. But I'll know for sure in a minute."

"You're really beginning to worry me."

The phone rang.

I answered it.

The answer was the right answer. I came back.

"I hope your passports are in order," I said, "because we're all sailing the day after tomorrow on the Montmartre. For Le Havre. And in case you care, we have the biggest suite on the boat deck"

Tom said, "How the hell did you do that?"

"I won't explain until we're all sitting at one of those sidewalk places on the Champs-Élysées, preferably Fouquet's. The truth is, I can't explain right now. But this is all on the level. We're booked. Start packing."

Twit-Twit said, "He's as nutty as a fruitcake. He can't get time off from the magazine like that."

"Of course he can't," said Betsy. "But just in case he can, I'm going to start packing."

"On the level," said Tom. "Who did you call?"

"On the level," I said, "I can't tell you. I don't have influence like this, usually. But right now I do. And so we sail the day after tomorrow. After that, nothing but fun and frolic—and Dior and Balenciaga, and Maxim's."

That is how it started. Nothing but fun and frolic.

Oh, brother!

THE EARLY TRACES

"Now is the dramatic moment of fate, Watson, when you hear a step upon the stair which is walking into your life, and you know not whether for good or ill."

—Arthur Conan Doyle
The Hound of the Baskervilles

CHAPTER 1

The Last Arrival

As you will have gathered, the *Montmartre* was, at the time, the newest and most beautiful and most desirable and hardest-to-get-on ship in the fleet of the Compagnie Générale Transatlantique. She had, in fact, been in commission only five weeks.

But, two days later, we were standing on her promenade deck, looking down on the faces of those who were massed on the pier below to wave and smile or weep farewell to the fewer and luckier ones gathered on the decks above.

The final gongs had sounded moments before, and the last of the people who were going ashore were going ashore. We'd had some guests in the suite who'd come down to see us off, and after the usual toasts and handshakes and cheek-kissing they had left, and now the four of us were by ourselves. The trip was about to start.

Ostensibly, it was an ordinary departure of four people sailing to Europe, and for three of us it was. Twit-Twit was standing next to me with slightly moist eyes (why do women always get emotional at sailings and weddings?); Betsy and Tom would shortly begin the pleasurable process of slowing down, of realizing they were to be on shipboard for the next five days with nothing to do but enjoy themselves.

I was glad I'd been able to arrange that, especially since I am normally anything but a big arranger, and I knew that what I had done meant a lot to them.

I looked around. Tom looked healthier already. The TV show he produces had had a good year and was ending the season with fine ratings, whatever ratings mean. But it had taken a lot out of him, and that had showed.

Now he looked happy under the implausible Tirolean hat which he has worn ever since I've known him, which is fourteen years. But the white brush was missing from it, lost perhaps in the crush on the dock as we came through. Or perhaps in the crush in our suite, for there had been quite a few people, most of them armed with champagne.

"I'll be damned. I guess I've been kicked out of the Alpine Mountain Climbers' Club."

"I always knew you would be. But what for?"

"It must be because of that day I was supposed to climb a mountain, and goofed. I climbed a valley instead." Tom likes champagne.

"That could happen to anyone."

"Of course. But it was pretty dumb of me. I should have realized much sooner why the blood was rushing to my head."

We all chuckled.

The stewards came around again with their trays of paper streamers and bags of confetti, and we all took some and began throwing them down on the pier, and calling to people we spotted, and getting that feeling of imminence that seizes you at a sailing. Only one gangplank remained in place, and only two lines—at bow and stern—bound us to the North American continent. Those, and the hundreds of little paper streamers, still being flung downward with enthusiasm.

I suppose they symbolize something, the knowledge that you are going a long way away, and leaving a lot of people and relationships—ties that will soon be broken.

It's not such a bad feeling.

But Twit-Twit's eyes still were moist. So were Betsy's.

I looked to my left. Next to me was a little group of college girls—maybe I should call them a murmuration—obviously on their way to the long summer-educational tour of Europe. They were apparently under the chaperonage of a tall, dark young woman who looked like she might need a chaperone herself in due time. The girls had the well-combed, well-scrubbed look that American kids have and which you never appreciate for what it is until you've been abroad awhile and run into it in places that aren't well scrubbed.

But they weren't murmuring now or saying much at all. Some of them were dabbing their eyes, and again I thought, what in hell goes with women that they get so emotional when they leave land to go on water? But it happens, and it doesn't happen when they take planes.

Down below some blue-clad dock-workers came forward to lower the last gangplank. Only two lines and the paper streamers now held us to land.

I wondered if my assignment, if I may use the expression, was aboard. I'd been watching the gangplanks as best I could and had seen no sign of her. Maybe she'd gotten on early, of course. Or would arrive at the last minute; it would probably be one or the other.

I had checked the tentative passenger list when we first came aboard, and of course she was not listed. But she would not be traveling under her own name.

Maybe it would turn out she wasn't on board at all. In which case this would be an unalloyed pleasure trip for me. Otherwise I would have work to do.

The gongs were whanging their final warning. I spotted one of our friends in the throng below and waved to him. He waved an empty champagne glass back at me; he'd walked off the ship with it full. The dockmen began pulling the gangplank back.

Either she was aboard or she wasn't. I sort of hoped she wasn't.

One of the college girls was crying openly; probably her parents were down there in the crowd. Or a boyfriend.

Then I got my answer.

From behind us came a sudden wild explosion of sound. Everybody jumped. The ship's band had assembled behind us and, without even a warning roll on the snare drum, now broke loudly into "The Poor People of Paris." And even while the trumpet and trombone blared, and the clarinet and violin squealed and squeaked, and the cymbals clashed, a little black-coated figure came scooting out of the crowd below toward the lowering gangplank and said something to the dock-workers who were handling it.

You could see their exasperation even from where I was. But they reversed the motion, and the gangplank moved back into position. The lady in the black coat, sunglasses, dark hat and all, ran up into the ship, and the gangplank again receded.

She looked like somebody's frightened maid.

But she wasn't. There was no mistaking that figure and those legs.

My assignment was aboard. Oh, well. In a way, I felt relieved. At least our presence on the ship was justified to the guy who had arranged the transportation.

The ship's whistle sounded its farewell blasts. The band swung into "Anchors Away." The first of the remaining two lines was twitched aboard. I got an idea.

Without saying anything, I turned, ducked past the band, and headed topside to the boat deck. That's where her cabin was to be. I got to the stairwell just as she did, preceded by a steward carrying a small bag for her. I turned aside for them to pass and followed up the stairway.

In a long black coat she seemed a small, almost slight figure. Certainly not the most famous female body in the world. She wore small, thin-rimmed, tinted glasses, not the usual Hollywood-type of big frame sunglasses. Little tufts of homely, grayish-white hair wisped out from under the pulled-down black slouch hat. With no lipstick or other make-up, she looked more and more like somebody's old nanny, breathlessly making the boat at the last minute.

I had to hand it to her. From what I knew, she must have doped out that disguise herself and put it on herself. And it was pretty good.

They stopped at a stateroom door lettered B-78, and I brushed past without looking twice. Down at the end of the *Montmartre's* boat deck there's a tiny bar, primarily I suppose for the carriage trade that occupies the boat deck. I went into it because I wanted to get out of sight, and to appear to have been going someplace, in case I was being observed.

It also occurred to me that a drink would not be a bad idea at this point; I had not had much champagne because I don't like sparkling wines.

But the bar was crowded, and I felt a little nervous about leaving the others on the deck below. The ship's whistle sounded the final blast. So as soon as I thought it was safe and I was not likely to be spotted, I started back down the passage toward the stairs. I wanted to go by her door again to be sure I knew its exact location.

Just as I passed, the door swung open wide and the steward came out. I caught a glimpse of what was beyond. A girl who had just taken off an old frump of a coat, and was taking off a hat that had covered what seemed to be gray hair. The hair was gray all right. But the body and the young profile were known around the world. I looked away fast and kept going.

* * * *

"Where did you go?" Twit-Twit said.

I saw the last line snake inboard. The band was still playing "Anchors Away" but as the chorus ended they modulated without missing a beat into "Le Marseillaise." I looked down over the rail. Only the little ribbons of paper bound us to land, and they began parting. Dirty brown water appeared in the gap between the ship's white side and the pier. Confetti fell into it. The band played even louder, and people began yelling meaningless final greetings.

"Take care of yourself!"

"Have fun in Paris!"

"Kiss Marie for me!"

I told Twit-Twit, "I just went around on the other side. To see what I could see."

"And what did you see?"

"The other side. But I have to run below in a moment. Gentleman's powder room."

"You do not. You hardly touched the champagne. You'll stay here while we go down the bay."

"I'll stay for a little." She took my arm.

But for once I wasn't thinking of her. I was telling myself I knew where I stood. The subject was on the ship and I knew where to make contact.

The charm, as Macbeth's witches crooned, was wound up. The fact she was aboard was the signal that she was really going ahead and making the moving picture.

How long I could keep the whole thing concealed from my three traveling companions, I had no idea.

Still, perhaps because of the pleasant hysteria of sailing, I felt confident and happy. There'd be a drink soon, and then a delicious lunch. The rest of the day would take care of itself.

* * * *

The ship had backed out into the Hudson or North, a term I prefer, River. The band played a final brave chorus and then moved off to its next station in the first-class lounge. The tugs swung us around efficiently and pointed us south, and there was New York's West Side skyline. The Dolans were looking at it.

I said, "Look, cookie pants. I've really got to go below and see about our accommodations. Let's meet at the smoking room bar. Order me a very dry Martini. Like the nice bitch you are."

Unexpectedly, she squeezed my arm. "I don't believe you for a minute. You're up to something. And I don't know what it is. But I'll find out. And meanwhile, I love you for getting us on this boat at the last minute. It's going to be a dreamy trip."

I was glad that she loved me, for that or for any other reason. But I had gotten the accommodations at the last minute only because I had accepted a responsibility, and I had to do something about it now.

I kissed her cheek. "The bar. Ten minutes. A *very* dry Martini."

Below, the passages were filled with stewards bringing, late-arriving flowers and fruit baskets, and bearing away the glass debris from *bon voyage* parties. I went to the purser's desk.

"The final passenger list is not made up?"

"No, *m'sieu.* In an hour perhaps. Meanwhile, there is the temporary list."

"May I look?"

"*Mais oui.*"

I looked up cabin number B-78. It was occupied by Constance Kent and maid, Klára Vörös. Constance Kent. Why had she picked a name like that? Did she know of an earlier Constance Kent? (The Case of Constance Kent is one of the most teasingly uncertain murder mysteries in the unparalleled annals of English crime. Constance was a daughter in a family living in Wiltshire. Her mother died in 1852 after many years of emotional instability; her father married again, and on June 30, 1860, the body of Constance's four-year-old brother Francis was found, his head virtually severed from his body, in an outcloset. In the Victorian police investigation which followed, suspicion attached to sixteen-year-old Constance, due in part to the disappearance of a nightdress. She denied knowledge of the murder. In a highly controversial trial, she was acquitted and went into a French convent where, in 1865, she confessed that she had murdered her little brother because of hatred of her stepmother, whose child the victim was. But there was, and still is in certain quarters, suspicion that Constance Kent made her confession to help someone else. Sentenced to penal servitude, she was released in 1885, and disappeared in the fogs of anonymity. There is reason to believe that both Charles Dickens and Wilkie Collins drew on the case of Constance Kent for *The Mystery of Edwin Drood* and *The Moonstone,* respectively.)

But I had learned what I wanted; it was time to get to the bar.

CHAPTER 2

How to Succeed in Business—One Way

I got there by going out on deck. The skyline was still going by; we were passing the Wall Street district, and the sun was bright and the water sparkling.

I went up one deck too many and so walked aft in the open along the boat deck's narrow space, hemmed in on one side by lifeboats and by the windows of the deluxe staterooms on the other. As I did, the deck door of one of the staterooms opened and she came out.

The long black coat was gone. She was wearing a white bare-shouldered sundress and big, dark sunglasses. The hair was still faded silver, but nothing else about her was faded. She had the happy, relaxed air of someone about to enjoy a little quiet, after a hectic time. Which I guess was the case.

It was as good a chance as I might have all day, short of walking up to her door and knocking.

As she started to pass me, not looking at me at all, I said, "Procedural meeting."

She looked at me for a fraction of a second out of the corners of wonderfully sky-blue eyes, and went on.

I turned after her. "Procedural meeting," I said, louder.

This time she turned, and really looked at me. Then she went on again.

"ABC," I called. She kept going.

And a voice behind me said, "D, E, F. What the hell are you up to?"

It was the last person on earth, or rather on water, that I wanted to see at that moment. It was Twit-Twit.

"Nothing. Why aren't you at the bar?"

She had come out of a passageway door. "Because I thought I'd find out what was delaying you. Since when did you start molesting gray-haired old ladies?"

"I wasn't molesting gray-haired old ladies. I was practicing my spelling lesson."

"You were like hell. You said something to that woman."

Sometimes the most distracting thing you can say is the plain truth.

"I gave her the code word," I said.

"Go code-word yourself," said Twit-Twit. "And you know what word I'm thinking of."

"Come off it."

Twit-Twit is too smart a tactician to press an advantage once she has gained it. She said, "Come in and get your drink."

But as we walked down to the promenade deck, she added, "Don't think you're fooling anyone, junior."

The only people at the smoking room bar were the Dolans and a dark, sallow man with a droopy, Stalin-like mustache, although others were still at some of the tables nearby. The man with the mustache had a bright-blue shirt and the look of a weasel who is momentarily sleepy, and I concluded he was fairly drunk. Two Martinis stood in front of two bar stools, and Twit-Twit (In case you wonder, as a lot of people have, why she is called Twit-Twit, it's because her last name is Twickenham and, as explained in *The Traces of Brillart*, when she was in school some of her classmates nicknamed her Twit-Twit because they thought she was flighty and brainless. How wrong they were.) and I climbed onto the appropriate stools. That put me next to the sleepy weasel.

I sipped the Martini. It was still very cold, and clean, and dry. There's something about the first drink of the day, and I winked my appreciation to the bartender. He smiled. It still looked like the beginning of a good trip.

Tom was saying, "My glass is empty. Why is my glass always empty?"

Twit-Twit said, "There's a little leprechaun who keeps boring holes in the bottom of it."

Betsy snorted. "There's a big hole in the top of his glass," she said, "and a little leprechaun named Dolan keeps finding it."

Tom pushed his glass to the smiling bartender. "It's the story of my life," he said.

The sleepy weasel lurched in my direction and said, "How's everything?" I said it was fine and turned to Twit-Twit. But it wasn't that easy.

"Think we're gonna have good trip?"

"Sure. Why not?"

"I never been on this boat before. Any big boat, that matter. I always fly."

Twit-Twit murmured in my ear, "You make friends so easily. How I admire the gift."

"Go code-word yourself."

I turned and surveyed the tables and the few who had not already gone down to lunch. One man, sitting with a slender, dark-haired girl whose back was to us, looked like a real case history. He had not bothered to take off his dark cap or his sunglasses, his hands were encased in immaculate white-mesh gloves, and he wore a short-sleeved sport shirt with a gaudy tie. He continually turned a sort of bold, unblinking stare around the room in a way suggestive of a periscope.

"We have interesting traveling companions," I told Twit-Twit.

"We sure do, and I've got a little suspicion you're going to turn out to be the most interesting of them all. Honey."

"I've already told you what you can do."

"If we're going to have another, let's get it and then go below. I'm starved."

"So am I." I waved to the bartender.

"I may be seasick," the guy next to me said. "What's it like when you're seasick? I never got seasick going to Catalina or Avalon. Now I think I will be."

"Drink cognac and water, don't look at the horizon, and forget about the possibility," I said.

"You're a doctor?"

"No." The drinks were in front of us, and Twit-Twit and I reached at the same time and gulped at the same time. "I can make enemies fast, too," I told her. "Hang around and see."

"No, don't," she said. "He's tight. How about *dejeuner?*" she asked the Dolans.

"They sure pick up the patois fast on these foreign schooners," said Tom. "Let's go." He scribbled the suite number on the check, and we slid off the bar stools.

"Well, what business are you in?"

I don't like being rude, and I wanted to defer to Twit-Twit as much as I could.

"Magazines," I said, and followed her toward the door.

As we passed the man with the white-mesh gloves, I noticed he was holding a glass containing some kind of yellowish liqueur like Strega or chartreuse.

* * * *

We had asked for a table for four when we first came aboard. The maître d'hôtel took us to it. It was in a cornet of the dining salon and was one of the best tables in the room. Twit-Twit looked at me.

"I suppose you did this, too."

"I suppose I did."

"Do you have stock in the line?" asked Betsy.

"I own the line."

But I wondered how I had really done it.

Next to us was another table for four. There was a little, elderly man with cottony hair and a continual good-humored chuckle, and a rather gaunt, dark younger woman who was evidently his wife, sitting with another couple who were rather nondescript except for the man's glowing Technicolor tie.

The steward approached us. Behind him was our waiter; hovering behind him was the server, and not too far in the distance, the sommelier. You must admit there's nothing like French dining service.

The steward said the chef was offering a very nice cold *caneton à l'orange* in aspic, or if we wanted something more hearty, the *boeuf bourguignon* was very good. We all looked at the menu which offered about thirty-five entrées, decided on the duck, with consommé first, agreed on Chablis, and were leaning back comfortably when a page approached the table next to us.

"*M'sieu* R. Pennypacker?"

He didn't pronounce the name very well, but I understood, nevertheless. Old Cotton-Hair nodded eagerly.

The page handed him a ship's cablegram, saluted, and left. Pennypacker—I could not believe that it was he—thumbed open the envelope, read the message, leaped out of his chair, and uttered a loud "Hey!" It brought around every head that was within earshot.

"Listen to this," he yelped happily. He was addressing the woman opposite him, but twenty other people heard him read, "'Beth today made you grandfather again. Boy, seven pounds eight. Everyone well. Congratulations. Doctor Maxwell.' How about that?" he demanded.

The people around broke into applause. So did the other couple at his table. So did we.

"A grandfather again," he said proudly.

"How many is that?" the other man at his table asked.

"Six," he said. "Six of the loveliest little chickadees you've ever seen in your life."

The consommé had arrived; the sommelier was pouring our wine. Tom raised his glass. "To the chickadees," he said. "May they live long and fly far."

Other people around us raised their glasses, too. The old man bowed his head in appreciation. It was rather touching.

We finished our broth, and he said, "I must really go up and acknowledge that cable. Are you finished, dear?"

She said what sounded like, "Yes, Richie."

Tom said, "Congratulations, Richie," and the old man waved happily.

As the waiter and server held their chairs for them, the other man at the table asked indignantly, "How are our steaks coming?"

As they left, I noticed that Mrs. Pennypacker clung to her husband's arm and limped markedly.

After they were gone, I told Tom, "It isn't Richie, it's Reggie."

"Reggie?" Betsy paused in mid-forkful. "It sounded like Richie."

"Because you don't know who that is."

"Who is it?" asked Tom.

I dropped my voice. "That's Reginald Pennypacker. The industrial spy. I can't believe it." I never meant anything more in my life.

"The what?" said Twit-Twit.

"Skip it for now. Until the other people at his table have left. Then I'll tell you. At least, as much as I know. But that old sweet lump of kindliness is one of the most fantastic sons of bitches in the United States."

"And with that cliff-hanger you leave us?"

"Only for a while. What else is new?"

Tom said, "Well, the *Daily News* had an interesting story this morning on page 3, if anyone saw it."

I had.

"Merrilee Moore is missing," said Tom.

Betsy looked up. "You're kidding."

"I am not. She had contracted to make a picture in Greece. She came to New York three days ago from Beverly Hills to fly over. Then she disappeared."

Twit-Twit said, "Merrilee Moore can no more disappear than Mount Everest can. It's a publicity stunt."

"I don't know," said Tom. "She's a funny dame. Shy. Quiet. Insecure."

"You know her?" said his wife with the overtones of all wives.

"I've met her. Keep your hair on."

"I hadn't heard."

"It was on my last trip to Hollywood. A few of us had lunch."

"With Merrilee Moore?"

Tom will play the long-suffering husband just so long. Then his patience runs out.

"Well," he said, "there was a girl at the table. As I recall, the initials were M. M. And it was not Marjorie Main."

We all ate duck a moment.

"She's a doll," he added. "Who knows? Maybe she's on this ship, right this minute. Crossing by sea instead of by air."

It was time to change the subject. The people at the Pennypacker table had left. I said, "Now I'll tell you about Pennypacker."

"What's an industrial spy?" said Twit-Twit.

"Well, it's an interesting and very new profession," I said. "You know about international spies."

"I've read Eric Ambler."

"And John Le Carré. Well, an industrial spy is the same thing, but a little more localized. And considerably better paid. It goes like this."

I leaned back and watched our server bring us individual pots of *filtre*.

"Supposing you're a manufacturer, making a product that retails at fifty dollars and grosses twenty million dollars a year. And you discover that your nearest competitor is about to bring out the exact same product, or even one better, to sell at $39.50. You know production costs for this gadget, marketing costs, everything. Yet your competitor is about to beat you by ten dollars on the same product. Your twenty-million-dollar business is going up the flue. What do you do?"

"Buy a hot-dog stand," said Tom.

"What *do* you do?" asked Betsy.

"Two things. First, you recognize that your competitor has discovered some process that enables him to make the same product cheaper and better. Second, you hire an industrial spy to find out how he's doing it. There are only three or four such people in that business. The best, far and away, is Reginald Pennypacker. He's raised company-spying to a fine art."

"How do you know?" said Tom.

"If he'd talk, he'd make a whale of a magazine story. And after all, I'm a magazine writer. So I tried to do a story on him more than two years ago. I never got any further than talking to him on the phone a couple of times. He sounded younger than he looks, incidentally. I think he actually wanted publicity, but he also knew that it was not good for his business. Staying under cover is important to him—obviously. I've never even seen a picture of him."

"Well, you must admit," said Betsy, "you could hardly find a more unsuspicious old guy."

"He looks like Uncle Wiggly," said Twit-Twit.

"The secret of his success," said Tom.

"But how does he really operate?" asked Twit-Twit.

"By boldness. For example, a metal-processor has worked out a new and better way to treat steel, and his competitor wants to know how he is doing it. They call in Pennypacker, and old Reggie spends a week or more in the plant of his employer, learning this particular branch of steel-processing. He is of course briefed on what to look for when he gets into the enemy plant. Then he gets in."

"How?"

"He has a million ways. Maybe he claims he is a union representative. Or a big bidder for the product. He has occasionally pretended to be a police captain, looking for a holdup suspect, and asks the management to let him tour the plant so he can spot his man. Once, for stage dressing, he bribed a real patrolman in a Midwest town to drive him to the plant gate."

"Then?"

"He spots what he needs to spot. Maybe he pretends to be a camera fan and takes a few pictures. More often the camera is hidden in his tie or belt buckle. Anyway, he gets what he wants. And for a high price. Who'd suspect a lovable old grandfather?"

"You've got to hand it to him," Tom said. "Think he'd stand still for a TV interview next fall?"

"He'd be crazy to. But maybe he would, if you let him keep his back to the camera. You'll have the chance to brace him on this trip. Keep one thing in mind, though."

"What?"

"He doesn't always operate according to law. Like the kidnapping. Two years ago."

"Is this a joke?" said Twit-Twit.

I said, "Remember how Three-Kay oil was introduced? The manufacturer leaked news of the new automobile crankcase oil they had developed well in advance of its actual introduction."

Tom said, "Sure he did. For the sake of publicity."

"Right. Then suddenly you heard nothing about the product and it didn't appear on the market for a year. Why?"

"Why?"

"Because the process that made the new oil possible was developed by one engineer at Three-Kay. Only he could map the production process to manufacture it in quantity. Three-Kay had a competitor who didn't want to be caught without a similar product. The competitor hired Reggie."

"What happened?"

"Two things. The development engineer who had invented the new oil disappeared. For six months. In that time the competitor learned all Three-Kay knew about the new oil. They learned the process and how to duplicate the equipment. When Three-Kay came out with their new ten-thousand-mile oil, the competitor had the same thing."

"By golly, that's right," said Tom. "I even bought some of it for that Jag we had then."

"What happened to the engineer?" asked Twit-Twit.

"He had been kidnapped. For six months. Very comfortably. He wasn't tortured, or anything. The story is that he was flown to one of the smaller Greek islands, where he was given every benefit and courtesy.

"But for six months he was a prisoner, constantly guarded by three men—hired by Pennypacker, presumably. Meanwhile, Pennypacker went to work personally. When the competing firm had caught up with Three-Kay's research, the engineer was flown to Athens in a private plane and dropped off at the airport. He was even handed ten thousand bucks for consolation. A few days later he showed up in Dallas.

"With as wild a tale as you can imagine. But subsequent investigation proved he was telling the truth. He had been on the island he described, and they even found the house where he had been held."

"And little old Uncle Wiggly did that?"

"No one can prove it. But in certain circles he gets the credit. His retainer, just for consultation, before he ever lifts a finger, is twenty-five G's. And it's paid, gladly."

"I wonder what he's doing on board," said Tom.

"Probably just on vacation," I said.

"Let's go topside," said Betsy.

* * * *

We took the elevator and went up and out on deck, and got some fresh air. I looked north. You couldn't see Long Island, but we were probably nearing the Hamptons.

Then, because we were all a little tired, and well-dined and wined, we decided on naps, and went to the suite.

This was two bedrooms and a little living room, and we had arranged that Tom and Betsy would have the big bedroom, and Twit-Twit the smaller room with upper and lower bunks. I would use a sort of day bed in the parlor.

I had complained that this was not very companionable, but had not won much attention. Not that I expected to.

When the others had retired I stripped to my shorts, hung up a few suits from my bag, and then I lay down on the day bed. For a little while I could not get to sleep, perhaps because of the *filtre*. Anyway, I lay there thinking of how suddenly the whole thing had happened.

As I did, I heard a scuffling at the door and saw an envelope push under the doorsill. I got out of bed and picked it up. It was addressed to me in a feminine handwriting.

It said, simply:

"ABC—Starboard boat deck tonight at ten."

It was signed "M. M."

Things were starting to work.

* * * *

Perhaps this is as good a time as any to tell you as much as I knew myself at this particular moment.

CHAPTER 3

A Little Badminton

Newton Harlow III and I belonged to the same athletic club.

He belonged because his family had been charter members since the club was founded more than eighty years ago. I had belonged to it a year and a half because I had been elected and admitted, for reasons obscure to myself. But we both played squash and badminton at about the same speed, and for the past year Newt and I had been getting together to play once or twice a week, when his banking or my newswriting did not interfere.

I suppose in odd ways we admire each other. Newt thinks it is ludicrous, but I hope worthy, that a man can make a fair living by just going places, talking to people, and then writing about it. And I think it is both absurd and wonderful that a man can make a handsome living by computing the interest on large sums, borrowed or loaned, in sixteenths of a cent.

On the day we had had dinner at Twit-Twit's, Newt and I played three games of badminton singles at the club and retired, sweating and puffing, to the dry-heat room. There we sat, draped in brief towels and enjoying, or at least enduring, the heat.

He seemed oddly quiet, especially considering that he had beaten me handily two games to one. I wiped perspiration from my eyes.

"You won't do that again. I'm on to that new serve."

He grinned a little. He knew what I really meant. For a guy who is a highly dignified young banker and has battled his way well up in a world of facts, figures, and cold decisions, Newt is warmly perceptive.

"I am worried," he said. "I admit it. That's one reason I felt like a game today."

"Federal Reserve kicking you boys around again?"

"No. Not at the moment. But the movie business is."

"Movie business! Don't tell me your bank, of all the conservative, mossy, old-line banks, is getting into—"

"We are."

He looked around cautiously, although except for us the heat room had been empty ever since we came in.

He said, "Six months ago we loaned Mel Compton ten million dollars. Two months ago we let him have five million more. I was one of those who favored the loan. Now the money may go up in smoke. Greek smoke."

"Explain yourself."

"Don't think I can't. You know what Compton's done. Four successive hit pictures in two years—the hottest director—producer in the business. Each picture was low budget but it netted far up in the millions, and they're all still making money."

"I know."

"He came to us with a proposition. He wanted to make a big-budget picture, and had an unassailable proposition. He had arrangements with both the Turkish and Greek governments—he's a Turk, you know; Compton's not his real name—to make a super-spectacular based on Helen of Troy. And he had signed up Merrilee Moore for Helen. He had everything except that much money. It would be the first movie loan our bank ever made but, after some very sober meetings during which we considered his record, we decided to go along. He got the loan. And when he came back later for the other five million, he got that, too."

"So what's the trouble?"

"Merrilee."

"What's the trouble with Merrilee?"

I thought of her as I'd seen her in some of her pictures, and I laughed at my question. A goddess, a Circe, a taunting temptress, a lovely child, a warm woman...what could be the trouble with Merrilee?

"Nobody knows where she is," said Newt. He toweled steam off his face.

"Newt, are you crazy? A dame like that doesn't disappear."

"She has, though. In fact, as far as we can figure it out, I may well have been the last person to talk to her."

"For a minute I was afraid you were going to say 'see her alive.'"

"Oh, I don't think she's—she's met with foul play or anything like that. But—well, here's the problem. Maybe you can help. Come to think of it, maybe you could damned well help."

We both mopped perspiration.

"Merrilee worked for C-L-C Productions for almost ten years," Newt said. "As I'm sure you know. She's thirty-three now. At C-L-C she did drudgery roles. For years. Minor parts in B pictures at five hundred a week, and completely controlled by the studio. Then she got that good part in—what was the name?"

"*One Night on Fifth Avenue.*"

"That's it. Anyway, she suddenly went over very big, and the studio began to star her. Every picture she was in clicked, and she made millions for them. But the damned fools kept her tied to the same old contract."

"At five hundred a week?"

"Not quite. They upped her salary. But they still didn't pay her what she was worth. And she had no voice in what roles she would play, what pictures she would do—that sort of thing."

"So?"

"So when the contract's final clause was up, she cut loose from C-L-C, and especially from Roger Kane who runs the studio. Kane is a wild neurotic, of course. He has a fantastic temper. There's a story that he once had three psychiatrists working on him, all at one time, and finally fired all three of them the same day. When Merrilee quit he flew into a fairy fit of rage, called her ungrateful, and swore he'd have revenge. He even claimed he had been going to make Helen himself, and that Merrilee leaked the news to Compton. We at the bank know better, of course."

"This is a hell of a thing for a bank to have to deal with."

"Deal with! We're entirely underwriting the picture that depends on her alone. That's the rub. She's missing."

I was getting interested. "Maybe you'd better explain this in some detail."

"She came to New York to do some shopping before sailing. She and Compton, and another of our vice-presidents and myself, had dinner at the Colony. I've never been at a table so stared at by the rest of the restaurant. She was beautiful and ravishing and, superficially at least, bubbling with excitement. But I got the impression she was haunted by something. And the impression deepened afterward."

"How do you mean?"

"She was staying at the Carlyle. I offered to drop her off. But when we got there, she suggested a nightcap in the bar. I wanted to catch the 12:35 to Rye but—so. After a very healthy stinger, she told me what was bothering her. She was afraid of crossing the ocean. She had never done it before."

"*That's* why she was scared?"

"I don't think so."

"Then what are you talking about?"

"I don't know. But she was scared of crossing the ocean. By ship, air—or osmosis. She wouldn't say why. She did say she was thinking of taking the ship with a suitcaseful of sleeping pills and tranquilizers, and staying in her cabin all the way over and having her maid feed her pills periodically until she reached the other side."

"She sounds screwy."

"She is, but only a little. She's a reasonably balanced girl, Deac. On the level. But something deep was bugging her. Anyway, I made her promise to have another meeting, and she agreed. So, I took her up to her suite, and her maid let her in. Interesting woman, the maid. Hungarian, old, raw-boned. She's been with Merrilee for some twelve years and is devoted, I take it. At least, the suspicious way she looked at me gave me that idea. I said good night at the door and heard the bolt slide into place before I'd walked two steps."

"But what in hell is Merrilee afraid of?"

"Wait. Two days later she came down to the bank. She needed to arrange some currency transfers and things, and that was the excuse for having another talk with her. She looked like hell. She'd dyed her hair white, was wearing an old black dress, and I think had even made up to look older. Really an old woman."

"Why that?"

"I don't know. She said she just didn't want to be recognized by fans. But she'd gone a very long way to make sure of it. And of course she's been accustomed to stage make-up since she was a child. Anyway, she promised solemnly she would be on the *Montmartre,* and that her maid would be with her, and apparently a publicity man named Jones whom the Compton-studio people assigned to her at the last minute—not to get her publicity, but to shield her from it, if you know what I mean."

"I know what you mean."

"Jones was with her when she came down to the bank. He is not attractive, Deac. Shifty, loud—insincere and probably dishonest, in my opinion. You know those Hollywood types."

"Sure. But holy jiminy"—I started toweling my wet chest and shoulders for the last time—"all those Hollywood types are nutty. What does she really have to be afraid of? The ship sinking?"

Newt was staring into the corner. "Just fear itself, perhaps. Mutilation, maybe. She's afraid of something; that's for sure."

"But what does crossing the ocean have to do with it? And why the disguise?"

"I don't know."

"You're seeing sadists under the bed, Newt. Who in the world would want to touch a hair of the loveliest head—"

"Kane," said Newt. "Kane would. I think that's whom she's hiding from. You don't know how mad he is, Deac. And you perhaps don't know how he feels about women. He hates them. Even homely ones. Now the one whom a lot of people think is the most beautiful woman in the world has left his studio, and will make a picture for a rival producer, which will probably prove enormously successful. If it's ever completed, that is."

I got up and draped my towel around myself.

"Now you're sounding more normal. It's not Merrilee you're worried about. It's your fifteen million bucks. But it'll come out fine. She'll be a smash, the picture will—"

"Then why has she disappeared?" said Newt. "She's checked out of the Carlyle and no one knows where she is. She promised to be aboard the boat. But where is she?"

"She'll show up. How could she turn down a fifteen-million-dollar role?"

"I'm going to make you a proposition," he said. "It occurred to me before we started the badminton, when you said you had a month's vacation left over that you wanted to take now. I've been thinking about it while we were talking here. How'd you like to take your vacation in Europe, Deac? Expenses paid. And you'll presumably cross the ocean with Merrilee. In a posh suite on the *Montmartre*. Even bring a friend or two, if you like."

I will frankly admit that at this point I returned to the bench and sat down.

"Stop smirking," I said. "What do you mean, bring a friend?"

"I mean this." He was talking nervously. "Merrilee will be traveling with her maid. In a suite on the boat deck, as I happen to know. Jones—the publicity man—will be aboard, too. But the bank has a major suite reserved on the *Montmartre* practically every trip."

"The hell it does."

"For our officers. And preferred customers. It's part of the—part of the banking drill. The suite is also on the boat deck, incidentally, and we've held it in reserve simply to protect our investment—a fifteen-million-dollar investment. You could have it."

I laughed. "This is a new side of banking. Up to now I've always thought all you people did was send out notices telling us customers we were overdrawn."

"There are other sides. I'm serious. I couldn't be more so. I think Merrilee will be on the ship. If she isn't, God help everyone. Shooting starts north of Athens in less than two weeks. But I think she will be. And I would just feel our investment was more secure if someone like yourself was aboard, just standing by in the wings, so to speak."

"Why me? I'm no professional bodyguard. And ships have their own security systems, you know."

"Sure. The fact is, we have alerted the first officer, and well, frankly— paid him a little money. So, she'll be watched all right. And I doubt whether there can be any real threat at all, once she's aboard."

"She'll have Jones, or whatever his name is."

"I question his responsibility. He's just a press agent who was assigned to her a day or so ago. But having you there, just keeping an eye on her—well, you've been around and covered crime stories, and so on. To have someone with your savvy on hand—you wouldn't even have to spend any time with her—if you didn't want to."

"What do you mean, not want to?"

"Then why don't you do it? If a few thousand bucks over and above all expenses would—"

"Newt, for the love of God! I'm no private detective. I'll bet your girl is safer than a—a government bond. So's your investment."

"I don't think so."

"Then hire the Pinkertons."

I punched his shoulder, and we headed for the shower room.

* * * *

That's how it was until later that night when we had dinner at Twit-Twit's, and it turned out everyone wanted to go to Paris on the *Montmartre*.

I couldn't resist the temptation. For once in my life I could make a grand gesture.

So I made it.

* * * *

The evening before we sailed, Newt rang me and said he had finally heard from Merrilee—by phone, at least. She had at long last returned his many calls and, sounding very agitated and flighty, again promised she would make the trip. Newt had given her my name, told her I would be her general overseer, and said that I would contact her.

"Just as a precaution," he said, "I am going to send a wire to her on the ship, establishing a recognition code. You will be ABC, and the code words, when you first meet, will be 'procedural meeting.' Can you remember that?"

I said I could and privately concluded that Newt, the conservative banker, was letting theatricalism go to his head.

"I'm sure now that she'll be there, and I must say that I feel more relaxed," he went on. "Once she's aboard ship, I think we're safe. If you like, you could even see how the land lies before contacting her. But you should presently let her know you are there."

"I see. What about Kane? Might he be on board the ship?"

"I doubt it. To begin with, if he'd planned anything, I'd bet he'd get someone else to do it. I don't think he personally has the intestinal fortitude for any rough stuff. As I read it, it is her own fears that we mainly have to worry about. Well, bon voyage."

* * * *

Obviously she had received Newt's wire long after boarding the ship this noon or else had read it late. But now we were in communication.

Ten o'clock tonight.

I'd seen a lot of her films. I wondered what she would be like in real life. And what she really had to be afraid of.

CHAPTER 4

Procedural Meeting

That evening there was a little subdued dancing in the main salon after dinner, but only a little. As usual on the first night out, everyone was feeling quiet and receptive to an early bed and long sleep.

So we went into the smoking room, and the first thing I noticed was Pennypacker immersed in a bridge game with his wife and another couple. It gave me a dangerous idea.

Tom noticed something which gave *him* a dangerous idea, too. It was the ship's pool that had been just set up, a double one as a matter of fact, and most of the numbers had not been taken.

"That's for me," he said. "How about it, Deac?"

"I'm with you. What number do you like, Twit-Twit?"

She counted on her fingers. "Three. I do it by numerology."

The hovering steward came over, smiling, and I gave him a five-dollar bill.

"I like nine," said Tom. "What do you say, Bets?"

"I say you're wasting your money, you unlucky bum," said Betsy. "But if you want to lose it on nine, that's as good a number as any."

"The witch's curse," said Tom. "That'll win for me if anything will." He handed the steward another five and wrote Dolan after the "nine."

"You should have picked eight," Twit-Twit told him seriously.

"Why?" I asked. "Numerology?" Twit-Twit has a doctorate in chemistry and is about as superstitious as a theoretical physicist.

"There are eight letters in 'Tom Dolan.'"

I counted up. "And thirteen in 'William Deacon.'" I had never realized it before. "God, I'm cooked."

"I think you can get out of it," said Tom, "if you regard the thirteen as one-three and add them together. That gives you four. Then you're safe."

"And it doesn't hurt to take a little eye of newt and toe of frog just before bedtime, either," said Betsy. "You sleep all the better for it."

"Speaking of which," said Twit-Twit. "I was up at seven this morning. Shall we?"

As we walked out, I noticed Pennypacker chuckling over his hand and folding up a trick he had just taken. I wondered. I was being too intensive an amateur private eye, I thought, but still, I was supposed to be alert. And if Kane was planning anything, who was a likelier agent than Pennypacker?

We took the elevator up to our opulent suite. Walking in, Betsy said, "What a shambles this Deac got us into. But I suppose we can make do."

I grinned. I was a little proud of what we had. The living room, where I would sleep, had a French sort of mural along one wall, plenty of lamps, all sensible, and the furniture and carpeting were comfortable and deep. After some years of traveling on stories, my idea of comfort away from home is just good plumbing, a good bed, and prompt room service. We had a little better than that.

The Dolans waved good night, even though it was only nine-thirty, and went into their bedroom. Twit-Twit stood at the door of hers. My bed had been made up and turned down, and my pajamas lay across the foot of it. The light was on in the lavatory, and the window in the deck door at the end of the little hall that separated the bedrooms was half open. There was the comfortable feeling of vibrant forward movement which is one of the nicest things about being aboard ship.

"I'm surprised you didn't want a nightcap."

"A man doesn't always need a nightcap. I'm as tired as anybody."

She made a kiss with puckered lips.

"Good night."

"Good night, Twit."

I wasn't really sure what I was supposed to do, or supposed not to do. But, considering what lay in store, I had an idea that for the moment the best thing was to do nothing.

Her door closed.

I looked around the cabin. Fresh ice had been added to the bucket containing our last bottle of champagne. The wastebaskets had been emptied and my toilet articles arranged in the lavatory. My shirts had been hung in the closet with care, like children's' Christmas stockings.

Nothing beats traveling first-class super deluxe, I thought. Especially when a bank is footing the bill.

I thought of Pennypacker. It was still early.

I opened the door to the passageway softly and closed it softly. I walked downstairs one flight and glanced cautiously into the smoking room. Pennypacker was still there. I looked at my watch. It was twenty minutes to ten.

I didn't dare be late. Still—

I went on down to the main deck. There was a freshly mimeoed list posted next to the door of the maître d's office. I scanned it quickly and saw "Pennypacker, M-432."

I got out of sight and looked at my watch.

Nine-forty-five. I didn't have much time. What did I expect to do, anyway? At least, I'd see where he lived. And maybe a little more.

I walked along the narrow corridor on the port side of the main deck. I passed the little station where the stewards and maids stay. It was empty. Next to it was the little glass-doored case where you can, if you like, deposit your key when you leave your cabin, since it is always under the supervision of a maid or steward.

Technically, that is.

The key to M-432 was there. And no one was in sight, maid, passenger, or steward. I took the key.

I went to the door of M-432. I looked up and down the hall. No one.

I slipped the big key into the lock. It made a little noise. I tried to turn it. It made a lot of noise. A voice from within, rather hoarse, spoke out.

"Who's there?"

"*Pardon, m'sieu*," I muttered and hoped it sounded French. I pulled the key out, went down the hall, and turned a corner.

I couldn't tell whether it had been a man's voice or a hoarse woman's.

But I didn't hear a door open.

After a minute I walked back down the hall. No one was in sight still. I returned the key to its place and thought what a lousy thief I would make if I ever tried to become one.

I walked up to the boat deck and found the spot near her stateroom where I figured the meeting was to occur. Except for lifeboats, it was empty. My watch said one minute to ten. Our suite was on the other side of the deck and well out of sight, for which I thanked heaven. I started walking around the deck; she might have planned on another place.

It was a nice night. The sea was a little rough and especially up here you could feel the motion and roll, but it felt good. I'd not been on a ship for two years, and I suddenly realized that I had missed it, the strong steady press of the wind against your clothes and face and hair, the wet-salt smell, and the awareness that you were crossing the ocean as it should be crossed and had been for centuries, by lots of people more courageous than you—you with your pajamas carefully laid out on your bunk, and your well-ventilated suite, and meticulously served food.

I'd gone completely around the boat deck, moving quickly past our shuttered windows.

No Merrilee.

I stopped and waited, near her cabin door, and felt the wind's tug, and looked up at the night's stars.

Suddenly I liked where I was and what I was doing, and I realized that I had felt that way about what I had been doing for a good part of my life.

It's a nice thing to realize.

A shadowy figure brushed past me.

I turned. It was a bulky shadow, with a hooded head. But the ankles weren't bulky.

The hood turned slightly, and I knew I was being looked at.

"Procedural meeting," I said.

She came back slowly, like a dark wisp of fog on little cat feet.

I still couldn't see her face. Or anything else but the silhouette.

"Do you have initials?" she said in the husky voice that everybody in the world knew, and came closer. The hood fell back.

In that vague starlight, reflected by the ship's wall and lifeboat, the hair of dyed old-woman white became the pale silvery blond that has shone from ten thousand movie screens. The large blue eyes were still blue, but pale with anxiety. The profile could never change. Her little-girl's voice came breathlessly from lips always half-parted as though to drink in everything the world could offer.

"ABC," I said. "I'm also Procedural Meeting. I suppose you could call me PM for short. But my real name is Deacon."

"Oh, yes. That's what he said. The trouble was, I'd forgotten. Do you have a cigarette?"

"I'm sorry, I don't smoke. Should I get you some?"

"It doesn't matter. I'm better off without them. I smoke too much. It makes my voice husky."

Vive le huskiness, I thought. I'd never heard a voice quite so intimately provocative.

"So you are ABC."

"Yes. Really a guy named Bill Deacon. Magazine writer."

"Yes. That's what he said."

"Who said?"

"Mr.—that man. You know. The banker. I don't remember his name. Could I have a cigarette?"

For the first time I realized how nervous she was.

"I'll get some right away. What brand?"

"I'm sorry. I forgot. I don't really want one."

"Of course you do."

She had turned, and the faint light from the doorway showed her face, wide-eyed with chagrin and apology. At that moment I would have dived overboard to get one puff of smoke for her. But she put a restraining hand on my arm and so, I suppose, saved my life.

"No—I'm sorry. I'm a little rattled, I guess. I'm really better off without them, as I said. You're Mr.—Deacon, did you say?"

"Usually called Deac."

"I didn't think—you don't look like I thought you would. I'm Merrilee."
You sure are. "How did you think I would look?"

"Like Tony Quinn maybe. Or James Mason. Especially Jimmy."

"Sorry. I guess Eve always looked like this. By now I can't help it."

"I didn't mean that. You look lovely. A magazine writer?"

"Yes."

"I—I thought you'd be a private detective."

"I could learn to be a private detective. If it would help." It was the voice, I suppose, and eyes, and the little-girl's air of naivety. Anyway, I wasn't kidding.

"I opened the telegram late. I guess we met earlier but I didn't know what you were saying. *Procedural meeting.* I thought you were speaking French. Then after lunch I read the message that had come, and looked you up in the list of passengers. And now—here we are."

"Yes. What can I do for you? Get some cigarettes, I know."

"No. Don't. They make my voice hus—I said that, didn't I?"

"That's all right."

She studied me; she not only talked abruptly but acted that way. God knows what she saw. As for me, I saw the most beautiful face this side of heaven, trying to look old, which was impossible.

"Newt Harlow told me you were afraid of crossing the ocean. I'm here to help you. What can I do?"

"That's sweet. But nothing, really."

"What are you afraid of?"

"Nothing, really."

"Look, Miss Moore. I want to help. That's why I'm here. I know we just met. But—I want you to get to know me a little so you will trust me. That will make it possible for me to help you."

"You're sweet."

"Please stop saying I'm sweet. I'm not. I'm—I can be a fairly tough—tough guy."

"No. You're nice and you're not a tough bastard. That's what you were going to say, isn't it?"

Inwardly, I melted. I suppose I'm an easy melt. Outwardly, I tried not to.

"If you're not afraid of anything, why the disguise?"

She looked away, through an opening beyond the tarpaulined lifeboat, and watched the darkling sea.

I said, "Newt Harlow told me something of your problems. About the competition, I mean. But you're aboard ship now. Not much can happen here, can it? Who else is traveling with you?"

"Oh, plenty of people."

"Who?"

"My maid."

"Do you know her very well?"

"Klára has been with me for twelve years. Many years ago, when my mother was with a circus, Klára and mother were good friends and performed in a Viennese horse troop. Now she's the closest thing I have to a mother. Or any relative, for that matter. My mother died when I was sixteen."

And now you're thirty-three, although the publicity releases say twenty-nine.

"Anyone else with you?"

"Sad Sam. Jones, that is. My press agent, at the moment."

"I see. And why do you feel they can't protect you from what you're afraid of?"

"I'm not afraid! After all, I don't—I have nothing to worry about."

"Of course." I took her arm. "A turn around the deck?" I'd decided to take a chance.

"I'd love it." She stepped forward happily.

I waited for us to walk a few steps. Then, "What are you afraid of?"

I waited a couple dozen steps.

"You're nice."

"So you keep saying."

"It's something I don't like to talk about. Even with friends."

"Then you can tell me, because I'm a stranger."

She giggled. I don't admire girls who giggle. She giggled gracefully.

"It's something my mother told me," she said. "You see—I had an odd childhood. My father died when I was small. He and my mother were in show business. He was a magician, and she was his assistant. They were in vaudeville, or what was left of it. Movie houses, mostly neighborhoods, night clubs, even carnivals sometimes. After my father died, my mother worked up a mind-reading act with another man."

"And you traveled with them."

"Part of the time. The rest I lived with an aunt. But the mind-reading act was pretty successful. First they used simple word signals—you know the type. But after a while they learned to work silent."

"What do you mean?" She was beginning to talk spontaneously, forgetting herself.

"The silent code. My mother was the mind-reader up on the stage, and she was blindfolded, or so it seemed. The man she worked with—his name was

Ferdie—would go through the audience, saying practically nothing. He'd take things from the audience like billfolds, hats, watches, possessions, and say just, 'What's this?' and make her describe it. Then, 'This?' and 'This?' And so on. Sometimes even his back was to her. Sometimes he said nothing at all. There seemed no way they could communicate."

"But they did?"

"Of course."

"Then, how?"

Merrilee laughed, a tinkling pleased laugh, because she had mystified me.

"She could see through the mask tied over her eyes, which appeared to be a big black scarf. And he was giving her hand signals all the time. They worked out an elaborate system. But then—"

"But what?"

"A funny thing happened." We had reached a ladder leading to the bridge, and she stopped and looked out on the hissing sea. "I don't like to talk about it."

I waited.

"After a time my mother discovered that she *could* read minds, in a way. I don't mean she could do the act without signals. She never could do that. But she began to know things, other things, without knowing how she knew them. It was as if her concentration when she was on stage brought out something she always had, but never knew she had."

"For instance?"

"Well...There was the night in Buffalo. I was about ten. We were in this terribly cheap hotel and playing a crummy burlesque theater with the act. We were kind of broke. The weather had been terrible all that month. Ferdie and Mother had booked into the hotel as man and wife—it was cheaper that way, but it was really all right. You know what I mean. The truth is they didn't even like each other very much. But sometimes, when money was low, they had to take a double bed. That's how it was this night.

"Anyway, I slept in a little alcove off the bedroom, on a sort of sofa. During the night my mother took me into bed with her. I'd never remember it now, even though Ferdie grumbled considerably about there being three in the double bed. But I remember for what happened later.

"I dropped off to sleep, and suddenly I was waked up by a tremendous crash, like an explosion. The whole ceiling had fallen in on the alcove. It had been raining heavily, and there was a leak in the roof. Anyway, all this plaster fell on where I had been sleeping earlier. It could have killed me.

"The next day I heard Mother and Ferdie talking about it.

The ceiling fell down about four in the morning. But about one o'clock my mother had had this vivid dream, more like a vision I guess, really, in which she saw the ceiling fall on my bed, crushing me. It was so clear she could not get back to sleep. So she took me into bed with her. And a couple hours later the ceiling did fall. I would have been killed."

"Some people would call that coincidence."

"Sure. That's why I don't like to talk about these things."

"Things?"

"There were others. My mother *knew* things, sometimes. But if you tell people about them, they think you are crazy. Or that she was some kind of freak. I don't know why I talk about it now."

"Because you were going to tell me why you are afraid of crossing the ocean."

"Yes. I forgot. It's because of what went on between my mother and myself sometimes. Because for a while I knew things, too. Like once, when I was thirteen, and we were playing Boston at Christmas, and there was this store near the theater that had a wonderful red skirt for three-seventy-five in the window. I didn't tell anyone, a single soul, 'cause we were broke. As usual.

"But the day before Christmas Mother and Ferdie were talking and said we'd go out for Christmas dinner at the serve-self between the second afternoon show and the seven-o'clock curtain, and suddenly I said I'd wear my red skirt, and Mother said I didn't have one. But I said I would have, and I did. Later Ferdie asked me what I wanted for Christmas, and he bought it for me—he borrowed ten bucks from the theater manager, believe it or not. Ferdie was nice, sometimes. But the thing is, I knew I was going to have a red skirt in time for Christmas dinner. I don't like this."

She stopped.

"Don't like what?"

"I got the skirt. But while we sat eating Christmas dinner I knew that Ferdie was going away. I told my mother later. She said I was crazy. But on New Year's Day the act broke up and Ferdie went back to California."

"You mean you are psychic, too?"

"Not really. Although I know Mother was—sometimes. But me...I don't know. Like there's one thing I've been waiting for years to happen."

"What's that?"

She looked across the sea as we paced. Spray had dewed her long lashes. Finally she said, "There's a man with a green face. I find him hanging, by the neck...I can't see him clearly. But—"

"What are you talking about?"

"It's a dream I had—oh, fifteen years ago. I walked into a small room, almost like a closet or something, and this man was hanging there by the neck, and his face was green and drawn. He was dead."

"So what happened?"

"Nothing. Because it hasn't happened yet."

"There you are." I took her arm. She was cold and, I think, trembling. "Look. Everybody has bad dreams. Did you ever have a nightmare? A real one?"

"This is still going to happen someday. Klára says so, too."

"Who is Klára?"

"My maid. I told you. She knew my mother. Lately she's said she thinks I have my mother's ability. Klára is Hungarian." She said that as if it proved something.

We had come back around to her cabin, and the wind was stronger and colder. It was getting late. She'd be better off in bed and getting a night's sleep.

"It won't happen. Believe me. And let me tell you something. I believe in extrasensory perception. Anyone with a knowledge of what constitutes really scientific truth has to. There are people who can sometimes know things by means other than the accepted senses. Most scientists believe this today and accept the many years of tests made at Duke University."

"I wouldn't know about that. But I think it still happens to me."

"What does?"

"Knowing things."

"Such as?"

"Such as, why do I know that a few nights ago you were at a dinner that had something to do with me?"

The little coldness that went down my back had nothing to do with the night wind.

"You were," she said. "I see you. I think I saw you there when we first met tonight."

I know how easy it is to read this. Try hearing it firsthand, on a dark, remote ship deck, well out at sea.

I made myself say, "What did you see?"

"You were at dinner. At a small table. A few other people. A blond girl, I think. And wine glasses. And you did something. Yes—you made a telephone call. It was a—I don't know. I think of a pleasant, friendly dinner. But I was involved—I don't know, exactly..."

I said, "Well, of course I have dinner every night."

But I was in a little whirl. "We'll discuss this again. You still haven't explained why you are afraid of crossing the ocean."

"My mother. Less than a year before she died she told me that I must never go on the sea. I am going to die on the water, she said. I—I've never even dared go on a yachting-trip. You can't understand what it means."

She shrank toward me. I put an arm around her. She seemed glad for it.

"Do you know what I've been doing for the past three days? I've been staying in a suite in the St. Regis, trying to get up my courage to make this trip. I disguised myself—tried to look different—to escape from something. I don't know what it is, exactly. Do you think I'm crazy?"

"No."

"Do you think my mother was crazy? I don't. I tell you, she *knew* things. And she said when my time comes, it will be on water. That's why I was scared. And I *am* scared. It took three tranquilizers this morning before I even dared call a cab to get me to the boat."

Her head pressed on my shoulder. We walked in stride, saying nothing.

We got to her cabin door. "Nothing's going to happen to you. I promise."

"Oh, sure. But you know, I've never even learned to swim because of that. And I've posed in lots of bikinis."

"Swimming is the first thing you should have learned," I said. It didn't sound funny.

She gave me the key to her cabin door, and I started fitting it into the lock. As I did, I thought I heard a scuffling sound behind us. I looked around. There was nothing.

"I'm in B-15," I said, "just on the other side of this deck. If you need anything, call me at any time. I'm here to help. You know that." The door swung open. "And I can swim."

"You're sweet—really." She gave me her hand. I held it. I had an insane desire to kiss her. It really wasn't that she was pretty. I wanted to comfort her, and stop her from worrying, and make her realize that she was safe.

"Good night...Deac." I released her hand.

"Good night, Merrilee."

I heard the sound again, and belatedly looked around. It seemed to come from near the lifeboat.

From inside the cabin a hoarse, suspicious voice, neither male nor female, demanded, "Who is it?"

"Me, Klára. Back to sleep."

She turned and smiled into the light and said, "I hope I see you tomorrow," and she really damned near got kissed that time.

But I was a gentleman and just said, "You will," and turned and walked down the deck; and as I did, it seemed I saw the glimmer of a dark figure disappear around the corner at the far end.

I walked fast, but when I got to the turning no one was in sight. Then I returned to the scent of her perfume, which still lingered on the shoulder of my coat, and the warmth of her presence, which lingered even more.

CHAPTER 5

The Sleepy Weasel

After all that, I couldn't just fall into bed and go quietly to sleep.

I climbed a narrow, breakneck staircase to the sports deck, walked across the vague white markings for shuffleboard and deck tennis, and stood for a time at the rail looking astern toward the southwest. Somewhere, there below the horizon, Nantucket light must be flashing, and New England lay. Above me spread the dark, starry sky. Below was the black-and-white wash of our wake.

That had been quite a story. And told by quite a girl.

Toward the bow, two windows glowed in the cabin below the darkened bridge. That would be the ever-wakeful radio shack. Radio has always drawn me like a magnet. When I was a kid, one of my daydreams was to be radio officer on a ship. Not the captain, not the exec, not the admiral of the fleet—just the "sparks" talking to other ships, and to faraway places, and to home.

I crossed the deck and looked in a window.

It was half-open and a man sat under it, enclosed in a glassed-in booth, at a desk with a phone on it. He was talking on the ship-to-shore phone.

It was the sleepy weasel of the bar this noon.

"...just for a minute," he was saying. "She was just finishing her dinner. In her cabin...Sure, she seemed okay...No, don't worry about that, Mr. Harlow..."

I moved far enough from the window to be out of its light and still hear.

"...going to watch over that girl like a—like a mother hen. She's not the first star that Sam Jones has watched over, you know...Tonight? Tonight she was going to bed early, right after she finished dinner, and read."

She was, eh?

"And she's got that maid with her—you know...Okay, Mr. Harlow. Why don't I call you every night around this time? Give you a little report, so to speak...Right, Mr. Harlow. 'Bye now."

This was the press agent, then. And Newt Harlow was doing a little checking. On me?

I heard the receiver click and a chair scrape, and I moved back into the darkness beside a stack of deck chairs.

Jones came out of the radio office and walked briskly to the ladder. When his head disappeared below the deck's edge I followed on tiptoe.

I didn't know what I was doing or why. I was a little wound up, I suppose, and also suddenly aware that things were going on which I didn't know about.

Shadowing is a genuine art, and I've never had to practice it, but Jones made things easy for me. He headed straight for the bar where I'd seen him earlier. From the outside I saw him settle himself on the same bar stool and say something, probably the same thing, to the same bartender. Again there were few people in the bar. I walked in and sat one stool away from him.

I told the bartender "CC and water" and let my gaze wander around. Finally *we* noticed each other.

"Hi. You're the magazine guy, right?"

"Right."

"Editorial?"

"Right."

"Sure. I can tell editorial guys from advertising a mile off."

"I could be in the printing end. Or a layout artist."

He laughed. "Tell 'em a mile off," he said. "Have a drink."

"Got one, thanks. How do you tell them?"

"I been dealing with 'em all my life. I probably know a lot of people you know. I'm in public relations." He eyed me; the weasel look that he had lost for the moment returned now. "You know—a lousy flack."

"What's wrong with that?"

"It's a living—I guess. Gimme another pour, barman. How about you? Sam Jones is my name. I'm one of the Jones boys. With one of the studios."

"Bill Deacon. Glad to know you. No thanks, on the drink. One nightcap's my limit."

"Deacon. Sure. I know you. I read your magazine all the time. I know Bernie Welden."

Bernie's our Hollywood correspondent.

"Sure. Nice guy."

"He is that. You know"—he took a long pull on the fresh drink—"I envy guys like you. I've read your stuff in the magazines. Lot's of people's stuff. That's what I always wanted to be. A reporter. You've written some good stories."

"Flattery will get you anywhere."

"I mean it. Me—I got sidetracked into this lousy business. Years ago. I took it as a temporary fast buck." He looked into the bar mirror and even the walrus mustache seemed to droop a little. "I been fast-bucking ever since."

He sighed and sipped. "I guess that's why you always find me at a bar."

"We seemed to find each other at bars," I said.

"Then have a drink with me."

"No, thanks. Honestly."

He pushed his glass toward the bartender. "You going over on a story?"

"No. Strictly pleasure this time. You?"

"I'm working. I guess you'd call it that. Nutty assignment."

"Publicity?"

The weasel face grew momentarily alert. Then he shrugged.

"How'd you like to turn down ten thousand dollars?" he said. "In one-hunnert-dollar bills? That's what I did tonight. Just before dinner. Bribe money. And I coulda ask for twenny-five thousand and got it, too. And I'd turn that down, too."

"That's a lot of money."

"Sure it is. People think a press agent is a crook, always out for what he can get, willing to sell anybody down a river. Or up the river. Well, I ain't selling her—anyone, I mean—down a river."

He talked between steady sips, never moving the glass far from his mouth. I waited. He went on, as if someone had asked a question.

"Because I'm nuts about her, that's why. I need money much as any guy. Maybe more. But she's nice kid. I'm almost old enough be her father, but I'm nuts about her. And if you think I'd sell out...when I think what a nice kid she is...what's a lousy handful of hunnert-dollar bills?"

"Sure. Who is she?"

"No, you don't, pal. I'm a little stoned. But I can't tell you. I won't. Anyway, she's a long way from here."

"I see. Well, take it easy. And I'll take a rain check on that drink." I slid off the bar stool.

"You got one. You're smart, pal. Like I said. Like I shoulda been. I'm a little stoned. 'Night."

He wasn't the weasel now. He was just a defeated, middle-aged man, befuddled by life and, at the moment, liquor.

"Good night."

* * * *

The library door was still open as I went by and a man was sitting inside smoking a pipe over a book, the cover of which I recognized: *The Complete Sherlock Holmes*. He looked as if he enjoyed what he was doing. I went in and sat down. I wanted to think about what I had learned, and about how much I didn't know. I dropped into a deep leather chair.

But when books are around I cannot keep my eyes off them. In front of me was a shelf of reference books in both French and English, assembled for the passengers' convenience by a thoughtful ship line—dictionaries, a *Columbia Encyclopedia,* a *Who's Who,* Standard and Poor's securities manuals, and an athletic-record book. I took out the *Who's Who* and looked up Moore, Merrilee. She had an inch and a half of type which didn't tell me much I didn't already know, except that it reminded me of a few movies I had forgotten. I looked up Tom and was reminded that he had been born in Drogheda. I tried a couple of other friends to see if they had made it or were still there, and then, just for the hell of it, I tried Reginald Pennypacker.

He wasn't there, which did not surprise me. The only Pennypacker in *Who's Who* was a professor of psychology at a small California college, now retired. I tried the other spelling—Penneypacker—but there wasn't one. I put the book back. The man with the pipe still looked contented.

* * * *

In the suite I undressed, got into laid-out pajamas, turned out the bed light, and thought about Merrilee.

As I did, I heard people come down the hall, arguing. A man's voice came through our door: "Lousy damn food on these foreign ships. Lousy damned service!"

A key rattled in a nearby lock and a woman's voice answered him softly. The door slammed. Then, a subdued murmur continued behind the head of my bed. But I had recognized his voice. The couple who sat with the Pennypackers in the dining room had the suite next to ours. I looked at the luminous dial on my wrist. It was one o'clock.

I went back to thinking about Merrilee. She certainly had an effect on people.

It was a nice way to go to sleep.

CHAPTER 6

The Lifeboat

A brief, reserved jingle broke from the telephone on the bedside table. It made me conscious without awakening me. I looked up into darkness, then found the phone.

"Yes?"

"Mr. Dickens?"

"Deacon?"

"I guess so. This is Merrilee. Remember?"

Remember!

"I remember. What time is it?"

"I don't know."

My watch told me it was six-thirty-one.

"I'm sorry to wake you up. It's just that I'm scared. And you said—"

"I don't mind being waked up." I was gradually coming to. "What's the trouble?"

"I've been calling Sam. Sad Sam. My press agent. His stateroom doesn't answer."

Remembering how I had left him last night, I said, "He's probably just sleeping heavily. It happens, you know—after a tough day."

"But I think that's not like Sam. He's the nervous type. Except when he calms himself with Scotch."

"He was getting quite calm last night."

"But—oh, damn!" Fear made her voice shrill, and for the first time I became concerned. "I tell you, I have a feeling. Something's wrong."

After all, I was supposed to be earning my passage—our passages.

"I'll go around and look in on him. Then I'll report. What's his cabin number?"

"M-445. Do you terribly mind? It's just—I don't know what it is. A feeling."

I climbed into slacks and a jacket, and just stuffed a tie in my pocket. Going down to the main deck, I glimpsed the morning through a porthole.

It was gray and overcast, and the sea was tossing white spray. The ship was rolling a little.

M-445 was forward and I knocked smartly on the door. A steward appeared almost at once from one of those little housekeeping cubbyholes in the middle of the ship.

"*M'sieu?*"

"*M'sieur* Jones. Has he been up?"

"No, *m'sieu.*"

"He should be." I rapped again.

"Permit me." The steward came to the door and rapped a key softly on the key plate, in gentle reprimand.

"He wanted me to awaken him."

Another key rap, again gently.

"I wonder if anything's wrong," I said innocently. "If he is ill—" The steward turned a serious face to me. "Perhaps if you would just open the door," I said.

He looked uncertain.

"I won't go in, of course."

He opened the door. Over his shoulder I saw a turned-down bed and black pajamas arranged across the foot. The bed obviously had not been slept in. He went in and pulled the door to, without quite shutting it. In a moment he was back.

"No one in there, *m'sieu.* I looked all around."

"Thank you."

I gave him a dollar. But I wondered a little. Had Jones passed out in the bar? Fallen asleep in one of the salons?

The bar was locked tight. The lounges I walked through were vacant, except for one early morning letter-writer in the library. I went to Merrilee's suite.

She opened the door almost the instant I knocked.

"He's all right?"

"I'm sure he is. But he's not in his cabin. That's why you got no answer."

"Then where is he?"

She was in a white negligee. She had a newly lighted cigarette between her fingers. Her lips trembled and so did her fingers, so much that they shook the ash from the cigarette. For the first time her face looked almost as old as her dyed hair.

"Now wait a minute. It's not that bad."

"I'm sorry." She turned. "Klára!"

The maid appeared in the doorway to the bedroom.

"Make coffee, please. I travel with a little espresso machine. Maybe that will help things. I can't get over—I *did* get you up, didn't I? I'm sorry."

"I'm usually up early. Coffee sounds fine. I'll just put my tie on if—"

"Of course. Bath's in there." She pointed to a door.

But there were two doors, and I opened the wrong one. It wasn't the door to the bathroom, but led into a closet festooned with feminine coats and jackets. But above all, there was a strange bulk hanging from a high hook. It was a man's body, suspended by a length of heavy rope.

I don't know how long I looked at it. Then the ship's vibration slowly made it swing around, like a chicken hung by the neck in a butcher shop.

The bright-blue shirt and the droopy mustache I recognized right away. It was well I did, because Jones's face was not only strangely drawn and distorted, but it was a bright green, the color of young spring grass. The open eyes were hideous.

I made myself touch his wrist. It was as cold as the ice in the last drink I'd seen him sipping a few hours ago. I tried the fingers. They were rather stiff. Belatedly I thought of closing the door.

But a little cry came from behind me. She had come to the door and caught a full look at that green face.

"It's him!" she cried. "I've been waiting for it for years. Look at his face. It's what I dreamed years ago."

Her indrawn breath was the start of a sob. "My God, it's happening!"

* * * *

I have never come upon a dead body before and my first thought was that this could *not* be happening. I had known that there might be a possibility of trouble, but not anything like—

And then the second thought struck. She was not being theatrical; she was not putting this on. And yet why hadn't they found him before now? He was wearing the same clothes he'd had on last night. So he hadn't been to bed. When and how did he get here?

She had called him—at least, she said she had—and become alarmed when he didn't answer. But had he been hanging here in her closet all that time?

It takes long to say it, but not to reason it.

The maid came from the bedroom, a spoon and a can of Italian coffee in her hand. Her iron face never changed, but she put down the coffee, and Merrilee ran impulsively to her. The maid opened her arms as to a child and her big, muscular hands comforted slender shoulders. I saw the hard eyes shift to the open door, and she obviously saw what was hanging there. The expression remained as it was.

Then she put Merrilee in a chair, and made the coffee. As she did, I said, "When did either of you look into the closet last?"

Merrilee said, "I guess I did, a little before midnight. I took my sleeping pills out of that little alligator handbag. Then I went right to bed."

"And slept well?"

"I usually do if I take the pills."

"But you were awake early this morning."

"Yes. I don't know why."

"And you?"

The maid looked up from the espresso machine. "I tidy the place after my mistress. Then I go to sleep."

"Where do you sleep?"

She pointed to a day bed near the door leading to the corridor.

"And you heard nothing all night?"

"Nothing."

"Do you usually sleep soundly?"

She shrugged and began pouring coffee. She handed cups to us. I sipped thoughtfully. Then I motioned Merrilee into the bedroom and closed the door.

"Do you trust this maid?"

"She's been a mother to me for twelve years."

"I mean, is she devoted to you? Deeply?"

"I'm sure. Yes."

"I'm going to get that body out of here. And hide it."

"Why?"

"I don't know."

"Are you crazy?"

"Yes. Will she keep a secret for you?"

"Of course; she is fanatically loyal. She is Hungarian."

"I know—they go together."

I went out the door leading from the suite to the boat deck. Morning air, cold and clear, poured in, and the first thing I saw was the lifeboat near which we had stood last night. Beyond was another. And another. Tarpaulins were lashed over each, tied by intricate knots.

I walked to the far lifeboat and looked around me. Above, a shadow passed. I saw an excessively tall, thin man with a lean yellowed face striding the sports deck above, eyes closed, his hands holding a white handkerchief over his head with fierce determination. He looked like a Hindu. He turned and strode back out of sight.

I tried the nearest knot. After a time it came loose with sudden ease.

The Indian returned, continental heels clicking on the deck above. I shrank against the cabin wall. No one else was in sight. He turned and left again. I untied another knot and rolled the tarpaulin over.

The Indian's footsteps returned. I dodged back out of sight. The footsteps went away, and I ducked back into the cabin.

I said, "You two get into the bedroom. I've found a place to hide him."

When the bedroom door had closed behind them, I went to the closet, taking with me a knife which had come in a complimentary bowl of fruit.

But before cutting the body down, I examined as best I could the marks which the rope had made on his neck. I had to force myself to touch him. But I made sure that there were no small black-and-blue marks along the groove which the rope had made in the neck. That was of huge importance. Marks like that are made by the rupture of small blood vessels in the skin, but they can occur only when the person is alive at the time of the hanging. Jones, therefore, was dead when he was strung up.

I inspected his clothes carefully and saw no bloodstains. I swung him around slowly, and then saw what I was looking for. Blood had thickly matted the hair at the back of his head.

He had been struck a heavy blow, maybe two, which had slightly indented the skull. I suppose that must have killed him instantly. Then he had been roped up.

I sawed through the rope with the knife, supporting the corpse with one arm and, as the last strand parted, I heard the sound of heavy breathing behind me. Merrilee and Klára were watching me through the barely open bedroom door. I ruthlessly dragged him to the door leading out on deck. He was heavy and stiff, and his bulk made scrape marks in the carpet.

The Indian's loud walk rang out again overhead, turned and retreated. No one was in sight.

I dragged and lifted the body over the threshold, out onto the deck, and then—as fast as I could—to the lifeboat. I lifted the awkward bundle and pushed it across the gunwale into the boat, not caring how it tumbled. I pulled the tarpaulin back in place.

The Indian returned. I went back into the lee of the wall. He left, briskly. He was quite a walker.

I peeked into the lifeboat. Jones was mostly on his back and right shoulder, feet up. I tied the ropes hastily, as they had been tied before, in sailors' bowlines. I ran back to the cabin. The Indian was coming.

My coffee was still on the table. I drained it. The maid poured more. She seemed to understand something. Merrilee looked at me round-eyed but thankfully from the chair she had never left.

That painted face was no coincidence. Someone who knew her old fears—and nightmares—was playing on them with conscienceless cruelty. The enemy was aboard then, and not only aboard, but opening a ruthless war. And Newt had figured she would be secure once she was on the ship!

Yet even then I felt a pang for Sad Sam Jones. The poor guy had been well nicknamed, all right. But why had he been killed? As an object lesson? Because he had refused to be bribed?

I drank some more coffee. "How did you happen to call me?"

"Who else *was* there?"

And then I was glad I had done what I had, stupid as it might prove to be. At least it gave us time to figure some things out and might disarrange the plans of whoever we were fighting.

With the knife, I cut down the fragment of rope tied to the closet hook, put it in my pocket, and finished the demitasse.

"Better take another sleeping pill," I said. "There's nothing else you can do right now. Except lock both your doors when I leave."

I left by the boat-deck door. I hoped no one would see me coming out of the cabin.

I went down to the main deck by a circuitous route, deck stairs, the main stairway, stern-end stairs, a deck ladder. The only people I saw were a couple of elderly gentlemen in loud jackets and their ladies in bright sweaters, heading for breakfast.

I walked past Jones's stateroom and noticed an odd thing. Clipped onto every door, where mail or notices are stuck, was the morning's ship paper. Except on Jones's door. His newspaper was missing. I stopped.

I pushed it and the door, now unlatched, swung open. No one seemed to be inside. But someone obviously had been. And had even taken the newly delivered paper. To indicate Sam Jones was up and around? Or to wrap something in?

I stepped in and closed the door.

It was a small cabin, with a small bath and a sort of corridor leading to a bleak porthole. Obviously not one of the most luxurious accommodations. Not that it mattered now to Jones. The unused black pajamas were still laid out on the turned-down bed.

The bathroom held only the usual toilet articles. I didn't ransack everything in his two bags, but they seemed to have the customary articles, plus two bottles of Scotch. On a little table lay a letter, handwritten and unfinished:

My Dear Jan:

Was glad as always to hear from you but sorry about Harvey. Perhaps you're better off, honey. It looks like a bad marriage, but I'd rather have my daughter realize it, and start over, than go on living in the same old rut.

It goes without saying, as you asked, that you can count on me. Haven't you always been able to count on your father—or at least almost always? That time in St. Louis, maybe not.

I'm on an assignment which will pay well, although right now I'm fairly broke and will be for about another month. But knowing that you need money, I will send you at least $250 no later than three weeks from now, probably from Athens, unless—

It ended there.

"Unless..." It is an eloquent word.

I conjectured what trouble his daughter was in, and what he had planned to do for her. Whatever it was, he would never do it.

I left the letter where it was. I hadn't touched anything but the clothes in the bags.

No one was in the corridor. I left, wondering who had last been in there and had gone out so hurriedly as to leave the door ajar.

CHAPTER 7

A Knowledge of the Score

At a couple of minutes before noon, we were lying in deck chairs banked around the upper pool. For an April day in the North Atlantic it was more like a bright July morning, and some of the women passengers, especially those with good figures, had donned bathing suits and were getting a little early tan.

It was lazy and somnolent, but it could not dull the memory of what had happened earlier. Lying there, I thought of what I had done and how many people knew I had done it. I decided I was fairly—*fairly!*—safe. Neither Merrilee nor the maid had any reason to say anything, and I was quite sure I had not been seen by anyone, including the tall Indian. My only danger was the steward who had opened Jones's stateroom at my request, and I had worked out an answer to that, if and when the question came. I was quite sure no one had seen my second visit there.

"Going below a minute," Tom said, raised his tall bulk out of the chair, and left.

"Now what?" asked Twit-Twit.

"If that bum is getting himself a drink this early," said Betsy darkly, but she settled herself back in her blanket.

I returned to my thoughts. When would the question be asked? Would they find him at all? They must; there was surely inspection, as well as patrolling for stowaways. I couldn't keep my eyes away from the boat deck above us, where, out of my immediate sight, was the lifeboat and its stiffening cargo. I began feeling nervous again. Simultaneously I wished they'd never find him, and that they would find him right away and get it over with.

All morning I had debated going to the first officer, whom Newt said had been paid to help, and telling him everything. I had decided against it. The main thing now was to keep the opposition off balance while trying to discover who he or they were. The first officer could hardly help in that.

Tom came back unhurriedly.

"What took you so long?" said Betsy, who makes a point of treating him with exasperation because she is never exasperated with him at all.

"I went down to see who won the ship's pool," said Tom, dropping into his chair. "They were just getting ready to post the winners, so I had to hang around a minute."

Betsy looked at him. "And so?"

"I spent that minute at the bar," said Tom. "With a Martini."

"Tom Dolan! Without any breakfast? You had a Martini on an empty stomach?"

"Of course not," said Torn., closing his eyes comfortably. "My stomach wasn't empty. Because I had a Martini before the one I'm talking about."

I said, "And who won the pool, pray?"

"Oh," said Tom. "Somebody named Twickenham," and didn't even open his eyes.

Twit-Twit let out a shout. "Hey! On the level?"

"On the level. Number three the winnah, and you were on it alone. There's a hundred and fifty-five bucks waiting for you."

"Numerology and clean living always win," I said.

"Bets, we'll have lunch at Maxim's," said Twit-Twit. "By ourselves. Caviar and Montrachet."

"What did I say about clean living?"

"If you really did it by numerology," said Tom drowsily, "give me a reading, will you, pretty gypsy? I'm going to play the damned thing again tonight."

"I don't know any more about numerology than you do. I just did it by—by—"

"Woman's intuition," I said. "Or ESP."

"I don't know anything about ESP. And I don't believe in that, either."

"You don't?" I asked. "Why not?"

Betsy said, "Here we go."

"Do *you*?"

I envied Tom his stop at the bar. This had been quite a morning, and I didn't feel much like a debate. But Twit-Twit now was on one of the few subjects about which I have definite convictions.

I said, "Yes. I believe in ESP. I don't see how anyone who evaluates the evidence, even briefly, can do anything else."

"You sound half-serious."

"I'm more than half. The only difficulty with the concrete evidence proving ESP exists is that it is surrounded by an aura of fakery."

"Like what?" said Tom, not opening his eyes, by which I knew he was listening carefully.

"Like the old commercial spiritualists, who held séances in darkened rooms and levitated tables, or made horns blow, or put you in touch with your dead uncle. Or, in a way, the perfectly decent, wonderfully entertaining stage magician who saws a woman in half and tells you what card you will draw before you draw it—you know he is tricking you, of course, and you enjoy being tricked. ESP has nothing to do with any of these.

"Nor, for that matter, with the people who make a reputation by claiming and proving that there is no seemingly supranormal effect which they cannot duplicate by artificial means. This leads to a dangerous fallacy, by the way—that any natural phenomenon which can be duplicated synthetically is necessarily fake or nonexistent.

"It is like arguing that, since man has learned how to make real diamonds in an electric furnace, all the 'natural' diamonds found over the centuries are fakes. Or that, since high-fidelity sound reproduction can copy a violin's tone and timbre so faithfully that it fools even concertmasters, there is no such thing as genuine, live violin music.

"The fact is that the gift of ESP in some people, not regularly and not throughout their lives, but nonetheless definitely and *demonstrably* there, has been proven so often and so solidly down at Duke in Dr. Rhine's parapsychology laboratory that it makes ordinary scientific 'proofs' look like kindergarten exercises."

"Like for instance?" said Betsy.

"In many scientific procedures," I said, "it is accepted that if you run off a hundred tests of a thesis and they come out okay, you can consider your case proven."

"Well, okay. So what?"

"Take an applicant for an M.A degree, especially in the physical sciences. Say it's chemistry. He repeats his experiments, based on his thesis, a hundred times. It works ninety-eight times out of the hundred. That's good enough. Now he writes it all out, and that is his M.A paper that earns his degree. He has proved that when you do so-and-so, as in his experiment, it works."

"What about the two times it didn't work?" asked Tom.

"That could well be due to an impure chemical, faulty procedure, a dirty test tube, or whatnot. Ninety-eight times out of one hundred is enough for ordinary scientific proof. Even when you are doing the same simple thing over and over again. But Rhine has had people under the most rigidly controlled conditions call cards correctly to the point where the odds are millions or billions to one against such a possibility. And do it more than once. There was one case of a subject who was tested regularly at Duke and averaged close to ten correct calls out of twenty-five in a card-calling test which extended over two years. On one occasion, he called twenty-five cards in a row. To attribute something like that to mere coincidence is mathematically unthinkable. (As recounted in Dr. J. B. Rhine's *New Frontiers of the Mind,* the subject was a young divinity student named Hubert Pearce, and the odds against calling 25 cards correctly in a Zener deck are 298,023,223,876,953,125 to 1. Rhine studied a number of subjects at Duke who could consistently score 8 to 11 "hits" with the Zener deck, which has 25 cards equally divided among 5 different symbols. On the basis of mere chance, a subject might be expected to call 5 cards correctly out of the 25.)

"Personally I think the occasional ability of some people to demonstrate clairvoyance, telepathy and even precognition beyond a reasonable doubt has been proven. It happens, and maybe oftener than we think."

"What about people who have dreams that seem to come true?" said Betsy. "Aren't they coincidence?"

"I haven't been talking about dreams. I've been talking about laboratory tests. The dreams are usually set down to coincidence, yes. And I suspect that's what they often are."

"And other times?"

The hideous pattern of that green face would not leave my imagination. "I don't know. Sometimes in dreams or visions people see things they could not possibly know about. I don't know. Let's get off this."

Tom got up. "Okay, swami. Tell me, who's going to win the opener?"

"Opener?"

"The Mets and Dodgers are opening the baseball season this afternoon in Shea Stadium. What'll be the score?"

I pulled my blanket over me. "I'm going to sleep and dream it. Ask me at lunch."

"Come on, Bets. We're going to get in on that pool money before the good-money numbers are gone. Let's leave them here to sleep together. Doesn't that sound lecherous?"

"You're not leaving me," said Twit-Twit and got up. "I'm going with you," and "See you," to me. She was mad about something.

I pulled the blanket up around my face, closed my eyes and tried to forget everything for a moment.

I was snapped out of it by, of all things, a perfume.

At least I think that is what I sensed first. Then I heard a hoarse voice that roused me more because I had heard it recently. It said,

"...so we can get off Southampton. You know? In three days. I inquire. That is the first—what I mean—port of call."

"And then?"

"Then plane straight back to Hamerica."

"What good would that do?"

The first voice I had not been sure of. The second I recognized from its whispery breathlessness. Not to mention the perfume. I shifted my head farther down under the blanket. "It would get you off the ship. This ocean."

"My mother warned me against crossing the water generally. Not against ships. In a plane I'd still cross water."

"But it would be over fast, *kedves*" the maid said. "You wouldn't be dreading it again forever."

There was a silence. A new wave of scent engulfed me momentarily; Merrilee had shifted in her chair. So they had settled in the two deck chairs next to me. I wondered if they had reserved them for the trip as we had ours. It might turn out to be awkward.

Then she spoke, in a small determined voice.

"I'm not going to turn around and run. I'm not going back to America. I'm not going to be afraid all my life."

"Of course. But just think it over. And take another of your pills. Steward. Steward!"

But the deck steward, who had brought us bouillon and little sandwiches earlier, was not around.

"Or would you like a treatment—a quick one?"

"No. A green pill."

"I will get water myself for you."

A shadow fell across my chair, and I saw the maid's shouldery bulk move down the deck.

I pulled the blanket away. "Hi."

"My God. Were you next to me all the time?"

"I was napping," I lied. "Glad to see you out and about."

"I thought—we thought—a little air would—"

"Clear the air. Right."

I twisted around. Big steel-rimmed sunglasses, a low-pulled hat, and the blanket made her unrecognizable. It was almost funny, considering who she was and what she was, under the disguise, to glance across the pool at the eager young ladies in sun and swim suits, hoping they looked good.

"I think everything's all right," I said. "Just keep your mouth shut. And especially your maid's."

"Don't worry about her."

"I'm not worrying. No one saw me."

"He's still in the lifeboat?"

"That's right. We may all have landed and be off the ship before he's found." It was unlikely, of course, and I wondered what the ultimate morality of the thing really was. But in the meantime, she might as well be comfortable. "I doubt if there's any link at all between him and you. Did you and Jones ever meet on board?"

"No."

"Good."

I'd better warn Newt as soon as possible, I thought, not to make any radiotelephone calls to anyone aboard. "Don't take any personal phone calls, except from me, until I tell you. And tell your maid."

"Why?"

"I'm not sure myself. But I'll bet I'm right. And that I can explain later."

"All right. But I wish you'd not treat me like a complete child. In fact, I'd like to ask you a question."

"Go ahead."

"Do you think I have extrasensory perception?"

I wasn't going to answer that one truthfully.

"After this morning?" she insisted.

"I don't know."

"I told you about my dream before—before we saw him."

Yes. If you're telling the truth.

"Do you think my mother had it?"

"I don't know. I don't like to keep saying that. But how can I tell?"

"I think mother did. Klára wants me to go back to the United States."

"What do you want to do?"

"I want to go back."

"And?"

"I'm not going. In spite of what happened this morning. I've been afraid of too much too long. I want to find things out."

"You're right. So tell me something. Do *you* think you have ESP powers?"

"Yes."

The whole thing was getting too serious. Far down the deck I saw the maid returning, carefully bearing a little white cup of water.

"Klára thinks so, too."

"Okay," I grinned. "Who's going to win the opener today? Come on, princess. Use your powers."

She smiled, and in spite of the glasses and the hat and everything else, it was a smile that, had it been around at the time, could have melted the iceberg and saved the *Titanic*. "You mean the baseball game?"

"Yes. The Mets and the Dodgers. They play this afternoon. What will the score be?"

She looked at me oddly, a faraway look. The maid came up.

"Drink this, *kedvesem*." The maid glanced at me as if she had never seen me before.

Merrilee took the pill and gulped some water.

"Twenty-one to nineteen," she said.

I chuckled. "Better do better than that. This is major-league baseball, not the Little League. Twenty-one to nineteen is a football score."

"Thank you, Klára." She handed the paper cup back to the maid. "And nuts to you." But she smiled.

I threw the blanket back and got up. "Sorry. But don't take too many tranquilizers. There's a gala tonight, and it would take your mind off your troubles. Mine, too. First dance?"

"I don't think I'll go. After what happened to Sam—I didn't know him really, of course—but still—and I'm supposed to stay under cover. But thanks anyway. A lot."

As I walked toward a change of clothes and (I hoped) an unbelligerent lunch and (I knew) a rewarding drink, I thought to myself. I'd laugh if she turned out to be right about that score. Like hell I'd laugh.

A hand grabbed my shoulder and I wheeled nervously. "What do you want?"

It was Tom. He looked a little startled.

"We were wondering if you fell asleep."

"I did."

"Everybody's ready for lunch."

"So am I."

"You getting a little jumpy?"

"Not that I know of."

"Maybe I am. You know what? Notice that old dame who was sitting next to you, in sunglasses and so on. I could swear I know her from some place. As if she were somebody else."

"Now who's jumpy?"

CHAPTER 8

Method Actor

The clangor of alarm bells and a steady blasting of the ship's whistle sounded *abandon ship* that afternoon shortly before six bells, if you like nautical parlance. Or about five minutes of three.

All passengers filed up to the lifeboat stations and made little un-funny jokes and were very amused.

Everyone except me. For one thing, I wasn't there, and for another, I was not in a joking mood.

Since lunch I had been thinking the abandon-ship drill could give me an opportunity, which might not come again, to take a look at Pennypacker's cabin. His presence on board *might* be coincidence. He *might* also be working on something else. There were a million *mights*. But he might also be the unknown opposition.

A quick look at what was or was not in his cabin could resolve a lot of questions.

For, as I thought it over, I'd decided that if I were one who wanted to keep tabs on Merrilee, or scare her out of the trip and out of making the movie, I would want to bug her cabin and thus learn what might pass between her and her maid, or what she might say to visitors or phone callers.

I'd thought of this during lunch, which was rather quiet, partly because the weather after the morning sunshine appeared to be closing in, and the sea was beginning to heave, making the plates slide on the tables. Pennypacker had looked over as usual and asked how "you boys" were coming along, and we said fine; and then he had looked to the table on his other side and asked how "you girls" were doing, and the three schoolteachers sitting there said they were never better. They looked green. But that was about all the action. Twit-Twit was noticeably cool and seemed to be kicking up a personal storm of her own.

So, after lunch, I said I wanted a little air and went out on deck by myself and watched the college girls try to play Ping-Pong, despite the pitching, and that is when I made the decision, as well as what plans I could, for getting into the cabin. Just how I'd do it, or even whether I could, I didn't know; I could hardly hope to get the key again.

It would also take some nerve.

I acquired a little with an after-lunch brandy in the smoking room bar and while I sat waiting for the alarm, and arranging my strategy, such as it was, it occurred to me that at some point I had also better search Merrilee's cabin and see if it was bugged.

I lingered over the brandy. I wanted to be as late as possible. The pitching was getting stronger, even though the *Montmartre* is a big ship.

"Looks like we'll have weather," I told the bartender.

He shrugged a smile. "Sometimes it happens. It is too bad today, because of tonight."

"The gala."

"*Oui, m'sieu.* The dinnair. The dancing. It is too bad."

"People will still enjoy themselves."

"We will be stringing the—how you say?—lines, in another hour I think, *m'sieu.*"

He smiled again, but this time only his eyebrows shrugged. He picked up the tip. "Thank you, *m'sieu.*"

I knew what was in his mind. He was not supposed to talk about bad weather, or that there was going to be a storm.

That is when the alarm bells went off, and the whistle began to hoot. I looked at my watch as though I hadn't realized how late it was, though I'd been watching the time on the little ship's clock over the bar.

"Better get below," I said, and again sipped the brandy, and put it down as though I couldn't finish it all at once.

Of course our steward would presently notice my absence, when the head count was made and, from what I had seen of ships' drills, would start a check. Let him. That would take time, and all I really needed was a few minutes, given some luck.

I heard the murmur of conversation as people passed in the corridor outside on the way to their battle stations. The bartender was looking at me, respectfully but in silent warning.

I drained the cognac. "See you after the riot."

I went down the grand staircase, still killing all the time I could, and being bumped by those rushing to or trying to find their emergency stations. Some of them had already put on their bright-yellow life belts, frequently upside-down.

The clang of bells and the whistle hoots stopped. Suddenly the ship was very quiet and deserted. I found Pennypacker's corridor, and there was no one in it. Nor were there any keys in doors, or in sight. An officer appeared at the far end of the corridor, and I was inspired. Sometimes inspiration beats luck.

I quickened my pace and tried to look scared.

I hurried to Pennypacker's door and almost beat the officer there. He was bulky in a big yellow life jacket.

"*Pardon, m'sieu,*" I said in my superb French. "*La—la clef?* I—oh, I forget. Pardon, but can you let me in my room? *La chambre?*" I pointed to the door. "My key—*clef*—is inside. I need my—" I pointed to his life jacket—"the vest."

He looked annoyed, and barked "Hurry, *m'sieu.*" But he twisted a pass-key in the lock and opened the door, without really glancing at me.

"*Merci,*" I said.

I stepped inside fast, and closed the door. Only then did I think to look around and discover if anyone was in the stateroom.

* * * *

No one was.

Of course not. Being a meticulous old fuss-budget, Pennypacker would be among the first to line up on deck, laughing with his wife about how the life jackets didn't fit, or didn't become them, and making all the other old jokes.

Meanwhile, I had work to do.

There was a big suitcase of expensive soft leather opened on a luggage rack. I fingered through it quickly. Shirts of good broadcloth, a couple of pairs of slacks, underwear, handkerchiefs of excellent linen. A smaller bag under the rack contained shoes and two wrapped packages, which I guessed were presents for friends abroad or last-minute purchases. Two cartons of cigarettes. A snorkel—was he going to the Mediterranean?

I still hadn't spotted what I was looking for. The bathroom was next. Shaving things spread out below the mirror, pajamas and robe properly hung on the door, bottles of cologne. Nothing else—and no place of concealment.

Then I began to realize something was wrong. It scared me.

There was only one other door and I opened it. This was a closet, and hanging in it were a topcoat, two man's hats, and three suits that looked expensive. But nothing else.

That's what bothered me.

Where were Mrs. Pennypacker's things? This was a man's room—one man traveling alone. Did she have a separate cabin? Or had I made a real goof?

Was it Pennypacker's cabin? Or had I picked the wrong one in my haste to convince the officer?

The door to the cabin bumped behind me.

I leaped into the closet and almost closed it. A steward's capped head looked in, made sure the room was empty, and then ducked out. It was the usual routine check for the emergency drill. But I heard his key scrape in the lock and fasten the door firmly.

I was locked in.

But locked in where?

I felt cold sweat break out on my forehead. Honestly. You hear of it, you know, but I think this is the first time in my life it ever happened. For all I knew, I was shortly to be grabbed as a sneak thief.

I went to the door leading outside and tried the knob. The door would not open. I was trapped, all right.

There was a phone. I could call and get somebody to come—the entire ship's personnel couldn't be participating in the drill—and lie my way out. Maybe.

I moved toward the phone on the bedside table. I didn't know what I would say. But I had to say something fast. Before the drill was over and Pennypacker came back. If it would be Pennypacker.

There was a book on the bedside table. It was Maugham's *Ashenden*. A folded sheet of flimsy paper, a ship's cablegram, marked the reader's place. I opened the book; he had reached page 218. I opened the cablegram. It was addressed to Reginald Pennypacker, via SS *Montmartre,* and it read:

BOEING STOCK SHOULD GO TO 78 STOP
PLEASE ADVISE STOP
MURPHY STOP MERRILL LYNCH

I read it twice, absorbed it—as much as I could absorb—and put it back as I had found it. I reached for the phone. Then I saw something else.

It was a little black wisp that looked like a caterpillar on the gold-colored carpet. I reached down for it and, as I did, I saw something else. The corner of a black-leather bag under the bed. I picked up the wisp. It was insulation from a piece of cable, with a tiny section of copper wire still in it.

I was right!

The black-leather bag came out hard from under the bed; it was very heavy. It looked like one of those cases news photographers use to carry cameras, plates, film, and the rest of the equipment. I have had to lift and help with a lot of them in times past.

This one weighed far more. A small, strong padlock secured it, and I could not yank the cover up enough to see what was inside. But by the feel there were very heavy things, and I knew what they must be—little black boxes of efficient sound-recording, and overhearing, and probably reproducing, equipment. Little coils of wire, and batteries and—

This time the key made only a slight rattle in the lock. I expect my heart thumped more loudly.

I pushed the leather case back under the bed fast and could not think of anything at all. I sat down on the bed as the man came in.

I said "Hi," and grinned a little stupidly and told myself I had to act drunk. *Be a method actor, Deacon.*

The man I grinned at was a slender, well-tailored man with an imperious carriage, cold eyes under a sort of widow's peak, and an air of poise and sureness.

"What are you doing here?"

"Locked in," I grinned. "I got locked in. Came in looking for my friend Pennypacker. You live here?"

"I live here. What do you mean, looking for your friend Pennypacker?"

"Guy who sits next to us in dining room. I had a few drinks before lunch. A few others afterward." I moved toward him and breathed my brandy fumes in his face, thankful for the impulse that had led me to have the brandy. I wished I had had four more impulses.

I grinned sleepily. "Didn't want to go all the way up to boat deck for one of them—those God-damn life preservers. Thought I'd borrow one from my friend, Pennypacker. But some damn fool came along and locked the door."

If he thought to wonder how I'd gotten in, I was sunk. But he wasn't thinking of that; he was watching me with suspicious eyes, and thinking of something else.

"Guess I got in wrong room. Door was open and—"

He brushed past me, looked into the bath, the closet, glanced at the big bag, the smaller bag, and under the bed. He also looked at the book. He touched nothing. I thought of a sort of thinking machine that could also move itself around with sure decision. It didn't take him long to make up his mind. I breathed him some more fumes.

"I guess everything's all right," he said.

"Sorry, if I—I mussed your bed. Damned near went to sleep."

"What's your name?"

I could hardly lie about it, on shipboard, "Deacon. Bill Deacon. Sorry for the intr—intrusion. I'm in cabin B-15. Buy you a drink if the—that drill is over."

"No, thanks." He looked annoyed now, but not suspicious or uncertain.

"Deacon," I said, just to drive the whole thing home. "Bill Deacon. Buy you a drink, any time. Rain check."

"Okay. Thanks, Mr. Deacon." He opened the door. "See you later."

I started out the door gratefully, but a method actor to the end. As I stepped through the door, I said, "You didn't tell me your name."

"It's Pennypacker," he said.

Brother!

I was out in the hall. In a blinding flash of belated intelligence I realized what must have caused the mistake.

"Oh, now wait a minute," I said. "You're not Richie Pennypacker. I don' care who you are, pal, you're not Richie Pennypacker. That I know. 'Cause I know Richie Pennypacker."

"I am *Reginald* Pennypacker," he said stiffly. "I believe there are two Pennypackers aboard. Possibly more. Good day."

He closed the door in my face.

I walked down the passageway uncertainly.

What in hell had I blundered into? And while I had talked my way out of it momentarily, how long was I good for now?

CHAPTER 9

The Big News

The elevator door opened as I hurried along the corridor, and I lurched into it, just to get away from Pennypacker's neighborhood. Two old ladies, of the sort who seem to do most of the luxury traveling, were in the elevator. Both carried life preservers; the drill was over, then.

I hadn't made it, even tardily.

"...lot of nonsense," one of the old ladies was saying. "You know it as well as I, my dear. They do it just to make you think they're being efficient."

"Oh, I don't know. I thought it was exciting. Breaks the monotony, anyway."

"Well, if you're bored with my company, my dear..."

How long would Pennypacker believe my act?

The door opened at the promenade deck, and I stepped out.

I walked past the movie theater, its doors draped by heavy velvet curtains. I heard Merrilee Moore's voice say "I don't think we know each other, do we?" in cool, million-decibel accents. The afternoon cinema had started, and it was one of her pictures. There was no escaping her.

Walking on, I reviewed my accomplishments. In one day I had hidden a human body, a murdered corpse, in a lifeboat. I had probably loused things up with Pennypacker. And somehow I'd made Twit-Twit mad at me. A great day, so far.

Perhaps I should just jump overboard.

The tall Indian with the burning eyes passed by, glanced sidewise at me, kept going.

Then I thought of something about that body that had better be done.

* * * *

The radio shack was empty when I got there, which was good. It stayed that way, which was fine. We had advanced our watches an hour last night, so when the call came through it was five minutes after three in New York. The bank would have closed for the day, and Newt should be relatively free.

The radio officer signaled me into the booth, and I closed the door carefully and picked up the receiver. I wondered how these calls were monitored. Probably by tape. They were scrambled before transmission, I knew, and then unscrambled, or reconstructed, in New York. But none of it made a lot of difference if they were taped and someone had recourse to the tapes.

Then Newt's voice said, "Hi, Deac, what's new?"—and I had to improvise fast. We hadn't arranged a code for this sort of thing. We hadn't foreseen this sort of thing.

"That was an interesting conversation you had last night," I said.

"That I had?"

"Yes. The one you had."

"You mean with the boss? Here at the bank?"

"No, with one of our friends."

A silence. Then he got it.

"Yes, it was an interesting talk. But he's an interesting fellow, don't you think?"

"Yes, indeed he is. I think it's a pity that he has left the show."

I waited for that one to sink in, or explode. It didn't do either. There was a long pause.

"Left the show?"

"He is no longer in the cast."

I could feel Newt's alarmed uncertainty across nine hundred miles of ocean. "He—he has resigned?" he asked finally.

"He was fired. Permanently. Apparently by someone close to the manager of the other show."

"Jesus," said Newt, a man who I estimate does not use profanity three times a year.

There was a long silence which was eloquent, and not because it cost a lot of money.

"I thought you had better know."

"Yes. Thanks."

"This will create quite a sensation. However, it hasn't broken in the papers yet." I hoped he'd get that one. He did.

"No?" Newt isn't dumb.

"Only three people know. Now it's four, since I've told you. That's all. Except for the man who—discharged him."

"How is—how's everybody who knows taking it?"

"Okay—so far."

"Tell everybody to keep their chins up. This—now is the time for courage."

"It sure as hell is."

"Maybe I should fly to England in a day or so. You touch at Plymouth first, don't you?"

"Southampton."

"Maybe I should meet you."

"Maybe. But why don't you wait a day? I will call you tomorrow and keep you informed about—about how the show is coming along. And the cast."

Saying it, I thought of what had happened to the last guy who promised to give Newt daily reports. I looked up at the window, outside of which I had stood last night, spotting Jones.

You probably won't believe this.

There was a man standing at the window, watching me. It was getting dark outside now, because the approaching storm was darkening the sky and closing down the light, as if the Day of Judgment was at hand. But it was still light enough for me to see this man looking in at me, boldly, knowing that I saw him and yet not moving.

He had one good eye and one bad one, fixed motionlessly in a dead, meaningless stare that seemed turned on me like a mechanically directed ray. His dark coat collar, turned up around fat cheeks, concealed his face. His head was bare and bald.

"What's the matter?" said Newt in my ear.

"I better—I'll ring off now?"

"Is something wrong?"

"No. I don't think so, anyway."

I took a final look at the window. Dr. Cyclops took one last stare and turned away.

I said, "Just keep in touch with the—the latest theatrical news."

"Don't think I won't."

"And make all your calls to me only."

"I understand."

"You're my only link with the outside world. So flash me the instant you get any news. This thing has become rather sticky. To say the least."

We rang off.

When I walked out into the office, the window man had just walked in.

"I wish to make a call," he began, then saw me. He stared at me, silently telling me he didn't want to say anything in my presence, waiting for me to leave.

I thought of a two-word suggestion to make to him that would have given him something to do. But I didn't make it. That is, aloud.

As I moved across the sports deck toward the ladder, the wind tore at my clothes as though it had hands. The sky seemed to bend down over me and bare its teeth. I felt more than depressed and anxious. I felt alone and surrounded by uncertainty, and told myself I should never have left New York.

I looked back. Through the window I saw that Dr. Cyclops had moved into the phone booth. He was still watching me. He raised his hand above his head and pulled down a blind, giving himself privacy.

* * * *

When I walked into the suite, Tom hailed me from their bedroom.

"Deac?"

"Hi."

"Where the hell you been?" He came to the door. "At the movie?"

"No."

"We missed you at the boat drill."

"I missed you-all, too." I tried to make it sound funny.

He looked at me and said nothing. For which I was grateful, even though I knew what he must be thinking. "Everything all right?"

"Why not?"

"You look like a man who needs a drink."

"I always look like a man who needs a drink. Because I always do. Where are the girls, so to speak?"

"Having their hair done. Collectively."

"That should look nice. Are they getting their heads braided together?"

"Twit-Twit wrangled a hair appointment and offered to share it with Betsy. So I guess each will have half of her head done."

"And shave the other half? Very striking."

"You do sound desperate. Come topside. I'll buy you that drink. Besides, I want to get into the ship's pool for tomorrow."

"Thanks. I'm going to lie down for a while."

He paused at the door to go out. "You okay?"

"Why not?"

"You look kind of down. I wouldn't worry about Twit-Twit. You know women."

He went out and closed the door.

I lay down on the day bed and closed my eyes.

It was quite dark in the suite. The ship was vibrating noticeably, and I guessed that the engines had been revved up to hold her steady in the increasing sea. In spite of that, you could feel her walking end-to-end on her beam, a plunge forward and, after a moment, the long, slow rise and then down, the stern dropping again. The woodwork creaked and grunted and murmured. I listened to it and felt it, and tried to relax.

* * * *

I was roused by another sound.

It was human, in a twangy way, like the voice of a child or an old woman, who is weak and perhaps far off. It murmured something, audible above the ship noises, but not making words.

I waited, and it repeated. This time it sounded like two syllables, run together. I swung quietly off the bed.

The ship pitched and the woodwork groaned and a water glass in the bathroom rattled. I walked there on tiptoe. No one was in the bathroom. I went to the Dolans' bedroom. It was shadowy but empty. So was their closet. I went to Twit-Twit's smaller bedroom.

Her gown for the evening was stretched out on the bed, looking strangely empty without her in it, but there was nothing else. Closet and bath were both vacant.

From farther away I heard the voice again.

I went to all windows and looked out on deck. The tarps and lines securing the lifeboats snapped and strained in the cold gale. But no one was about. I thought of Jones's body lying in that cold.

Back in the living room it seemed darker now.

Then the small voice spoke more loudly, and I spotted where it came from: the closet near the door to the suite, where my clothes had been hung.

I moved to it on silent feet and put my hand out to the knob. But I hesitated.

The thought of Jones's corpse may have done it, or Merrilee's talk of ESP, or the man with the evil-eye stare. But I was a little nervous.

I took a deep breath, grabbed the knob, and yanked. The first thing I saw was something big and white; then two things big and white. They were paper sacks such as cleaners use to deliver your suits. I tore a ribbon of paper down one and saw my own dinner jacket. Someone had sent it out to be pressed for tonight. That was all.

Then something brushed my leg, and the voice spoke again, a kind of tiny scream, and I jumped a foot off the floor.

A small white kitten came out of the closet and was viewing me, with suspicion and indignation, from the middle of the carpet. It mewed once more in an oddly individual voice, and I turned on a lamp.

I began to laugh, mostly at myself. "You're a stowaway," I told her.

I picked the little cat up. She looked about three months old. I sat down and began to stroke her. She liked it and began to purr.

We sat that way for a while, and it was somehow restful and made me forget my worries momentarily. I wondered where she came from. I suspected she was a real stowaway. A passenger's pet would be lodged in the ship's elaborate pet facility.

"Pussy cat, pussy cat," I said aloud just as the door opened. "Where have you been?"

"Getting my hair done," Twit-Twit swept into the room. "Not that it's any of your God-damned—oh, *where* did you get that divine little kitten?"

"I bought it for you," I said. "At great expense. A present. Her name is Stowaway."

"Let me hold her—please."

I gave her the cat and told her the truth. I didn't mention how or why the kitten had frightened me. I like to put on a pretense of having average courage.

"Deac, is she really ours? She's so cute."

"I think she's hungry. I'll order some milk."

"Cream. And sardines."

"Why not caviar?"

But I felt better, punching the steward's button. Twit-Twit was coming out of whatever she had been in.

She took the cat into her room while I gave the steward the order. He was a handsome man with a face out of Raphael, but his fine soft eyes popped as I told him what I wanted. He came back with remarkable speed however, and I warmed the cream in hot water in the washbowl, while I cleaned an ashtray. I poured cream in it and knocked on Twit-Twit's door.

She had changed into a rather filmy housecoat that was decidedly eye-catching. She was cuddling the purring cat in her arms, and I put the cream on the floor and cuddled Twit-Twit a little. She didn't mind. Neither did I. It was the first good thing that had happened today.

"You'd better stop that. You'll give this little thing bad ideas."

"Well, you give them to me."

"We're going to let her eat."

She put the kitten on the floor, and it stopped purring, but it didn't imme-diately run to the ashtray of cream. Instead, it saw the edge of the housecoat and began pawing at it playfully.

"Look how she loves to play with the hem of my negligee."

"Who wouldn't?"

"Don't get sexy. Go drink the nice cream, dear." She picked the kitten up and put it in front of the ashtray. "By the way, how do you know this is a girl cat? Why couldn't it be a boy?"

"Don't get sexy."

The cat lapped milk. I nuzzled Twit-Twit's neck.

I said, "Does it make you feel kind of domestic?"

"That?"

"I meant the cat."

"Oh. The cat. What you were doing made me feel domestic. Or something like that."

"That's good."

The door in the living room burst open. Tom rushed in, and he was excited.

"Hey, you know what?"

"What?"

"Where's Bets?"

"Still getting her hair done," Twit-Twit said.

"Did you win the ship's pool so soon?" I said.

"Pool, nothing! Have I got—"

"Do you notice anything new around the room?" said Twit-Twit. "Like something drinking cream?"

"What are you talking about? Look! Do you know who's aboard this ship?"

I got a sinking feeling.

Twit-Twit said, "No. Who?"

"You remember that sort of old lady with white hair who sat near us in the sun this morning? With a sort of maid?"

"Yes." But she was now looking not at Tom but me.

"Well," said Tom, "I'm damned if it's not Merrilee Moore. In disguise—so to speak. But that's who it really is. The news is all over the ship."

And the little moment of respite was over, and fears and anxieties came flooding back, redoubled. Along with something else.

I could feel the chill from five feet away. Twit-Twit was surveying me as she never has before, not even the night I spilled red Burgundy on her new white evening dress.

She said, "So that's who it was, eh? And what do *you* hear from ABC, pal?"

THE DEFINITE TRACES

"Now, Watson, the fair sex is your department," said Holmes, with a smile, when the dwindling *frou-frou* of skirts had ended in the slam of the front door. "What was the fair lady's game? What did she really want?"

"Surely her own statement is clear and her anxiety very natural."

"Hum! Think of her appearance, Watson, her manner, her suppressed excitement, her restlessness, her tenacity in asking questions."

Conan Doyle

The Adventure of the Second Stain

CHAPTER 10

The Entrance

Dinner that night was a glittering affair.

Bright jewels glittered against soft flesh, of which a pleasant plenty was in view. The complementary champagne flowed glitteringly and often—to the delight of Tom Dolan, who persistently maintains that he hates champagne. The caviar glittered blackly and the male contingent, without glittering, was black-tied to a man.

Perhaps because a few decks down in the dining salon the ship's plunging was less noticeable, everyone was in a gala mood; even Twit-Twit seemed to have declared a truce, momentarily anyway. She looked pretty wonderful, incidentally, speaking of soft flesh.

Pennypacker—the cotton-haired one, that is, next to us—was beaming. "You boys care for a few hands of bridge after dinner?" he called over.

Tom gestured toward Betsy. "I've got to take her to the jig," he said, openly regretful.

"You don't 'gotta' at all, you ape," Betsy told him. "There are half a dozen men in the room dying to dance with me. Mostly ship's officers. Handsome."

Pennypacker laughed. "I'd like that myself. But I'm too old for that sort of thing."

I said, "You won't be too old until your grandchildren present you with grandchildren."

He laughed again and waved his thanks.

"Sometimes you can be nice," Twit-Twit told me. "Sometimes."

* * * *

I wondered what she would have said had she known that an hour ago, after dressing, I'd slipped out of the suite for a moment and around to Merrilee's cabin. I'd wanted to ask about her letting me search it.

But I found her in the throes of having the maid do something quite odd-smelling to her hair; now that she had been recognized, it was being changed back from the old-woman white of her disguise to the goddess-like gold that shone nightly on movie screens from Bangor to Bangkok.

So I said I'd see her at the dinner, and she smiled and said that would be fine and told the maid to let me in to do anything I wanted. I got back into the suite undetected.

Then we went to our favorite bar for a drink before the dinner, and the bartender asked me, "Would you like to try our new *spécialité*?"

"What's that?"

"It's a cocktail. The MM."

"What's an MM?" said Twit-Twit.

"Just this afternoon we learn Merrilee Moore is aboard. So I have the privilege of make a new drink in her honor. It is really a very *sec* Martini, madam, with a little drops of Irish whiskey in it. Would you care to try it?"

Twit-Twit gave me a look. She knows I love Martinis and also Irish whiskey.

When she spoke, her voice held a grindstone's warmth. "Surely *you* are going to have one, Deac." Her eyes were blue pebbles.

I gave her my warmest smile. "Not tonight. I think tonight I'll stick to my usual blackberry brandy and Coke, with banana slices floated on top and a sprinkle of cinnamon." Being French, the bartender had been genuinely shocked. I felt ashamed at having outraged him. I winked.

"A regular Martini," I said. "With an olive."

So I got over that hurdle.

* * * *

Now people were beginning to leave the dining room. The college girls and their chaperone went out chattering and looking like a walking bouquet of different-colored dresses. One of them had snagged a young ship's officer, and it was hard to tell whether he or she looked the more pleased. The old Indian also went by us. He wore a turban instead of a handkerchief, and his hot, wide eyes were fixed intently on something high above everyone else.

Tom said, "I'll bet he can do the Indian rope trick. Even without a rope."

I looked around. The dining salon was mostly emptying, but the other Pennypacker, the industrial-spy Pennypacker whose room I had burglarized, so to speak, was still lingering over his demitasse, stiffly correct, impeccable in dinner jacket, sitting at a small table by himself. Which, I guessed, was how he liked it.

The old-grandfather Pennypackers at the table near us were gone, but their dining partners were still at table. The man had had words with the steward because he had insisted on rare sirloin steak, even though everyone else had a special dinner on which the chefs had done themselves marvelously proud with lobster, tournedos, and crepes. So the troublesome couple had finally received their steaks and were grumping and chomping their way through them.

We got up. "Cognac?" asked Tom.

"Like a hole in the head," said Twit-Twit.

"I want no holes in your head," said Tom. "It's too pretty."

He patted her, and I chuckled. It wasn't the back of her head he patted. Twit smiled.

"Maybe a little cognac."

"But let's grab a table," said Betsy.

We went to the grand salon, and managed to get a pretty good table near the dance floor and fairly far away from both the bandstand and the little stairway down which you could make your entrance if you wanted to make an entrance. I wondered how soon I could excuse myself for half an hour and make my search.

When the liqueurs had been ordered, Tom leaned back in his chair. "That was a good dinner," he said. "In fact, more than that."

"You can't beat the French Line," I said.

"Damn right you can't beat the French Line. It reminds me of my undergraduate days in Paris."

Betsy said, "He's going to tell us about his undergraduate days in Paris. Just you wait and see."

Twit-Twit said, "Did he have undergraduate days in Paris?"

"I think he went to high school there. At the age of twenty-eight. He was backward. Never graduated, of course."

Tom told her what she could do, in a pleasant low voice. That was a good thing, because the salon now was filled up. They were beginning to set up extra tables.

"As a matter of fact," he said, "I lived for a year with a French family. That is how I learned about good food."

"Tell us about it," said Twit-Twit. She smiled.

Tom had had quite a lot of hateful champagne. "I will," he said. "And he did."

He looked at her. "The girls are getting prettier," he said. "And I am getting older. And I don't seem to be doing a hell of a lot about either."

"Drink your brandy and sober up," his wife told him.

"I will now tell you about my days in gay Paree," said Tom. "The truth is I worked like hell at the Sorbonne. But this family I lived with, it was honestly a gourmet's paradise."

"Really?" said Twit-Twit.

"Of course, really," Tom said. "To begin with, they always kept my room at a temperature that was perfect for chilling white wine. Then there was the lighting. It was ideal for growing mushrooms." Twit-Twit laughed. "And finally there was the landlady herself. She was a real charmer. She snuffled constantly, like a truffles pig, and she had the nose to go with it."

They kept bringing in more extra tables. "Besides that," Tom began. Then it happened.

The orchestra had just finished "*C'Est Magnifique*," and people left the floor. The drum gave a little preliminary warning roll. People looked up. A spotlight suddenly turned on from somewhere, hit the door at the head of the little staircase, and a girl entered, accompanied by a ship's officer. He wore lots of braid. But no one really saw him.

She wore a gown, shimmering white, that looked as if it had been enameled on her and made her fantastic body seem more tanned than it was. A single large star-sapphire glowed enthusiastically at her throat, as though it was overjoyed to be there, and its clear blue made her hair more precious than spun gold. But it was her face that made the entire room stop—suddenly.

She was smiling, a poised, proud, but friendly smile that said *I am glad to be here because I like you, and I think you like me,* and embraced everyone in the enormous room and took command of them, promising the men a great deal, and yet endearing her to the women.

She took the officer's arm and came down the stairs demurely and unaffectedly, and moved gracefully. Even the ship's creaking seemed to stop while she did.

Then, across the empty dance floor, the orchestra quietly struck up the theme from her last motion picture; and as she neared the captain's table, which was across the floor from where we were sitting, everyone suddenly, spontaneously, broke into warm applause; and she flushed a little and almost faltered, because she recognized its real meaning; I saw one woman's mouth tremble, as though she was going to cry. It occurred to me that, at that moment, there was not a man present who would not have lain down his life for her, and no woman who would not have given the rest of her days to be Merrilee Moore for that one night.

The captain himself—I recognized the oddly spaced stripes—seated her with a flourish, and everyone then tried to return to normal and look away. And failed, of course.

"Well, well," said Tom, "Anyone we know?"

"It isn't Marjorie Main," said his wife.

Someone tapped my shoulder. It was a waiter. "*M'sieu* Deacon?"

I managed to recognize the French pronunciation of my name. "*Oui?*"

"You are desired on the wireless telephone, *m'sieu*."

"Right. Thanks." I said, "Sorry" to the others. "Back in a moment."

Leaving the table, I felt Twit-Twit's eyes boring into my back, following me to see I didn't double back to the captain's table.

I didn't. I went to the radio shack, although I knew I could have taken the call in the suite. I sat down before the phone, pulled down the blind, and picked up the instrument. Newt's voice said, "Hi. Hope I didn't get you up."

"I'll say you didn't. We're having a very fancy ball. And guess who's there? As guest of honor."

"I've been thinking," said Newt. "That's why I called. It occurred to me—what's that? What was that you said about a guest of honor?"

"It seems Merrilee Moore is aboard," I said innocently, for the benefit of eavesdroppers of any sort. "She was traveling incognito, but she has been recognized. So tonight she made an entrance. And it was an entrance."

There was a pregnant silence. "I'm glad I called," he said. "This alters my thinking."

"Mine too."

"Is—is everything else the same way it was?"

"Oh, yes. There's nothing new in the papers."

"But there surely will be."

"Very possibly. But possibly not."

"That's what I wanted to talk to you about. I've been giving a lot of thought to flying to England. Now I'm sure I had better do it."

"Maybe so. There's even another reason."

"What's *that*?" He sounded alarmed.

It was not easy to say it without mentioning things I did not want anyone else to hear. "Listen, Newt. Listen carefully.

"I want you to call a girl at my office tomorrow morning. Her name is Madelyn, and she is a researcher. She and I once did a little preliminary work for a story on a man named Reginald Pennypacker. We never met him, and the story never came off. But I want you to ask her to get, as soon as possible, an exact description of what Pennypacker looks like—every possible detail and identifying mark—and cable it to me."

"I've got it. Will do."

"One other thing. Do you know of any way that—ah—my client could have learned about my telephone call to you that night, when I said I'd make this trip, while having dinner with some friends?"

"Why—why, maybe. I don't know." He sounded stunned. "I think I mentioned to her how it happened when I talked to her before she sailed. You remember, I talked to her only on the phone, and I said you had changed your mind at the last minute. I think I mentioned how, but only in a casual way. Anyway, she was so distrait and confused at the time that I really question whether she heard what I was saying."

Then that was the answer to Merrilee's ESP powers, at least as far as "knowing" I had had dinner with friends in some way that involved her. She had heard Newt virtually unconsciously, and then, when she met me and we talked, had consciously recalled what he'd said. As for the others that she described, she could have glimpsed us all together several times, once the ship had sailed. She wasn't really faking, in this at least; she was just self-deluded.

And right on some other things?

"Okay," I said. "That explains something. Thanks."

"Not at all." He sounded puzzled. "See you in Southampton Friday. And keep me informed if—if any news breaks in the papers."

"Don't think I won't."

When I got back to our table, I found yet another small table had been set up partly in front of ours for yet another couple. It proved to be the man with the mesh gloves, who was apparently squiring a fantastically striking girl. She looked like a harem beauty, with black flowing hair, a *café au lait* complexion and burned-sugar eyelashes, and I noticed that Mesh Gloves ignored her rather deliberately, and that she seemed to expect it.

"Everything okay back at the ranch?" Betsy asked.

"Yes. Sorry. It was the office, about a story I closed a few weeks ago."

It was an awkward lie, and what made it really awkward was that no one said anything more about it, and so obviously no one believed it.

The band struck up a tune, and I looked at Twit-Twit.

"Dance?"

"If you can tear yourself away from business." And then, as we got out on the floor, she added, "Whatever your business may be."

I put my arm around her much more strongly than I needed to. "My business is this. You smell nice."

"You gave it to me for Christmas."

"I have damned good taste. And speaking of business, I'm going to have to leave you again. For about half an hour."

"Why?"

"Don't flip. But it's better that I don't tell you right now. I will—and soon."

"It has something to do with Miss Moore."

"That's right. And it's making me bite my nails. Which is the understatement of the century. But it's nothing personal with her."

"I don't know why the hell I believe you."

"Just as long as you do."

I saw the Pennypacker who had caught me in his room—Widow's-Peak Pennypacker, that is—get up from a large table otherwise occupied entirely by the college girls. Their chaperone got up too, and Widow's-Peak followed her to the floor. They brushed past us presently. She danced well.

* * * *

I was sitting with my back to the dance floor, considering making my break, when someone leaned in on my shoulder and a familiar voice said, "Why don't you come over and meet the captain? He's a darling."

It was Merrilee, dancing with the proud and happy first officer.

"I'd like to."

They danced away.

"I'll bet you'd like to," said Tom.

"When did you get chummy with her?" said Betsy.

"Magazine writers get around," said Twit-Twit. "You know, they write stories."

"Or mash notes." I grinned. "Mind if I leave you a moment? I really should, and I can't tell you why."

"I can tell you why," said Tom.

"Shut up, you evil old man."

"I couldn't care less," said Twit-Twit, "but I'm going to try."

But she didn't seem really mad. So, a few minutes later I went over to the captain's table, and the first officer gave up his chair next to Merrilee.

"I'm glad I came," she said and patted my arm.

"To the party?"

"On the trip. I don't know that I should have come to the party." She lowered her voice and it became a fragrant breath blown in my ear. "I feel awful about Sam Jones, even though I hardly knew him. But I don't think I had anything to do with his death. Do you?"

"No."

"Why would he kill himself?"

"I don't know. Sometimes there's no logical explanation."

"And paint his face like that? He couldn't have known of my dream. I think it just shows that I do have some kind of ESP power. Don't you think?"

I ducked it again. "Precognition, it's sometimes called."

"You're like me. Mixed up about it. I mean—I don't know what I mean. But for days I've been scared and going sort of crazy inside, and tonight—well, tonight the way they received me and made me feel welcome—it just warmed me up all over. So that's why I'm glad I came. And you are responsible."

"I don't think I can take any credit."

"You can ask me to dance."

The band drifted into *Anima e Core*," a song that can make me amorous if I just hum it to myself.

Putting my arm around her on the floor, I felt a little self-conscious. I knew everyone in the room was watching me. She danced like a cloud.

"You look lovely."

"Never mind that."

"Tired of hearing it?"

"You never get tired of hearing it."

I saw the first officer go over to our table, bend over Twit-Twit, and she got up, looking pleased. As he led her to the floor, he looked a very quick question at me: he was being courteous and thoughtful, but was it all right? I smiled that it was all right, and felt grateful for French gallantry and quickness. He smiled back.

"I don't want to keep talking about Sam," she said. "He—he wasn't—well, a personal friend, you know." She had such a breathless way of talking. "But what will happen? His body hasn't been found. Will it be?"

"Maybe not."

Her arm tightened a little on my shoulder.

"Somehow I feel safe."

Maybe my grasp tightened a little too. "There's no reason why you should not feel safe."

"Oh, yes there is. It's what my mother told me. The sea. Like, I'm haunted by the idea of someone—of seeing someone fall overboard. Like a child."

"That's silly."

"It's not silly. It could happen. But it makes me even afraid of going near the railings."

"Why, exactly?"

"Because if someone falls overboard, I would feel I had to jump in after them. It would be—you know, a duty. To help them. And I wouldn't have the courage. That's what scares me. I'm a coward. I'm afraid of the sea."

I did hold her closer now. "That's really morbid. No one's going to fall overboard."

"It might be a child," she said, and looked up at me, and suddenly she was not beautiful and poised and glowing. She was fear-struck, and her fear was contagious. It brought back my own anxieties and responsibilities, so different and so much bigger now than when I accepted the job. "I would *have* to help a child. I couldn't let one die."

"You need a drink. A stiff one. No sissy champagne."

It was idiotic, but it is my own solution for sudden problems.

"Let's just get a breath of air," she said. "I'd love to go out on deck. With someone, that is."

"Okay. But after that, I'm going up to your cabin to try to get the lay of the land. As I said I wanted to."

I do not need to tell you, of course, that at that moment Twit-Twit and the first officer danced by, and I knew from Twit-Twit's chin that she had heard what we said.

And so it goes.

CHAPTER 11

Contents of a Lifeboat

We went out on the veranda deck.

The wind was strong; after a moment you could taste the salt on your lips. She took my arm and the ocean wind blew the scent she was wearing my way. It was dryly, understatedly pungent. I thought of her entrance and that elaborate hairdo.

"This may not do your coiffure any good."

"Klára can redo it in a few minutes."

It *was* cold, though. I thought of what she had on underneath that dress. Except her, there was almost nothing, obviously.

"Remember, I'm going to search your cabin," I said.

"Now?"

I wondered if she thought she was reading my mind. I wondered if she was.

"After a bit."

"Why?"

"I have the feeling it may be bugged."

"Who would do it?"

"That's a little hard to say." If she couldn't guess, why alarm her? She was having a good evening, and she deserved it.

"It *is* cold."

"Yes. In for another dance?"

"Let's. But you warm up with a drink if you like. I don't want one."

"I don't need one. I have on more clothes than you. At least, I think."

She smiled up at me and wrinkled her nose and somehow wiggled. Everything wiggled.

I dropped her off at the captain's table.

We danced and sat for a little while. Twit-Twit occasionally looked at me out of her eye corners, but she said nothing. We sipped brandy between dances and Tom went on about his student life in Paris and I occasionally glimpsed Merrilee, dancing with closed eyes and open mouth. At least she wasn't worrying about children falling overboard.

The friendly first officer, the one who had danced with Twit-Twit, came up to our table.

"*M'sieu* Deacon?"

"Yes."

"May I 'ave a word?"

"*Mais oui.*"

He led me out to a passage that connected the grand salon with a sort of serving pantry. Both were empty.

"*M'sieu?* You are a friend of *Mademoiselle* Moore?"

"I am."

"Something 'as 'appened."

He was being reserved, but his eyes were alarmed. Something *had* happened. I guessed what it was.

"A friend of *Mademoiselle* 'as—'ad an accident. Someone close to her. The friend 'as been found."

"Where?"

"In a lifeboat, *m'sieu.*"

I was right.

"Who—what happened? Who is this?"

"I don't know whether to tell her or not, *m'sieu.* The captain 'as commission—'as asked me—that is why, I thought, if you are a close friend, I would avail myself of your advice."

There were little windows in the swinging doors of the pantry entrance. Through them I could see the dance floor, and even as I looked I saw her for a moment, dancing with the captain, smiling, oblivious to the dark present.

"My advice is at your service. If it will help you."

"Perhaps you would tell her, *m'sieu?* Break the news?"

"Does it have to be broken? Now, I mean?"

"I do not *compre*—understand."

"She is enjoying herself. Look out there. Must we spoil her evening? Even though a corpse has been discovered?"

"A corpse?"

"A corpse. A body. The dead person."

He looked strangely at me, and for the second time during the brief period I'd spent on the ship I felt something cold crawl down my spine.

"*M'sieu,*" he said. "The person is not dead. Not yet, at least."

I don't know how long the millennium actually lasted, but during it I couldn't breathe.

"Perhaps you had better explain."

He said, "Perhaps you would be so good as to accompany me and see for yourself."

I said, "Sure," thickly, and followed him through the pantry to a service stairway and up a flight of stairs and then up some more and out onto the boat deck, all the time wondering what in God's name had happened.

For we went to a lifeboat. But it wasn't the right lifeboat.

The tarpaulin had been thrown back, and two men stood in the boat, one in a white medical jacket. They were struggling with something. A crewman, standing by attentively, snicked on a flashlight and shone it on a stretcher at his feet. The two men in the lifeboat raised something heavy. We both looked in.

The crewman flashed his light into the lifeboat, and we saw what they were lifting. It was a body, all right.

But it wasn't Jones's body.

It was the maid, Klára. She muttered something and her eyes rolled strangely under half-open lids in a way that did not suggest life as much as it convinced you of death.

"We'll take her to the infirmary at once," the man in the white jacket said. "If she lives that long."

CHAPTER 12

The News in Hungarian

"What do you think, m'sieu?" The first officer spoke in a low voice. "It is her maid, of course."

"Yes. I'd like to go to the infirmary with her and see if she can say anything."

"But *Mademoiselle* Moore?"

"There is nothing she can do. And there is plenty of time to tell her. I see no point in disturbing her at the moment."

"It is true."

We followed the stretcher-bearers and the doctor to the elevator, but we could not all get in, so the first officer and I walked down to the infirmary. While we did, I thanked my lucky stars that he had accepted me, as he clearly had, in the role of close friend of the family. I was desperately anxious to learn whether Klára would say anything, especially since I was sure the doctor's terse diagnosis was right. The head wounds I had glimpsed were actually skull depressions, deeply bloodied. They were sickening.

When we pushed into the infirmary's second room, white, bright, and antiseptic-smelling, she was stretched out on a sort of operating table. She had on a black maid's dress but the white cap was crimson and mashed into the head wounds. Her eyes were open and unfocused; her lips moved but only throaty, sucking sounds came out.

I asked, "Is there any chance?"

The doctor just looked at me. "The brain damage is massive. It's a wonder she's not dead."

"She cannot live?"

"I can do nothing, *m'sieu*. I have given her an injection. But I would not even touch that poor head. Adrenalin may keep her alive for fifteen minutes or a few hours."

"The wounds must be the result of a terrible beating," I said.

"It is clear she did not fall downstairs, *m'sieu*."

"Nor climb into the lifeboat by herself."

He smiled faintly.

"But can you guess at the nature of the weapon?"

"The weapon, I do not know, but a club of some sort. A heavy metal bar, perhaps. Wielded by *quelqu'un sauvage*."

I said, "Klára," a little loudly. There was no response at all. I bent over her and said it again, more loudly.

The eyes did not flicker. I smelled blood, the sweet, waxy, sickening smell that brought back major auto accidents I'd covered as a kid reporter, and once a horrible triple knifing. "She is beyond hearing, *m'sieu*."

"She is beyond everything."

"*Oui*."

"How was she found?"

The first officer answered. "The tarpaulin was not properly fastened by whoever put her in the lifeboat. It began to flap, and the bridge noticed. When a sailor went to fasten it, he saw her."

There was something suffocating, in spite of the careful air conditioning, about standing late at night in that bright room with all its helpless surgical equipment and useless cabinets of medications, waiting for someone to die.

"Will it matter if I try to talk to her again?"

They exchanged glances. "It will make no difference," the doctor said. "She is already dead. Except for ceasing to breathe."

I bent over her again, holding my breath.

"Klára. Klára*!* KLÁRA!"

Nothing.

"Who did this to you?"

I could hear the ticking of the big cheap watch on her wrist.

"Who did it?"

Then it came, a sudden gush of words, the eyes still open and sightless. But the words were strange syllables only. The high harsh voice was speaking in Hungarian. It repeated a phrase, and I grabbed a pad and pencil from the table and wrote it down phonetically.

"*Vezetö meg ölt engem*."

I listened carefully and wrote it down phonetically several times. There were minor variations, or so I thought. The watch ticked on precisely.

I said, "Is there a Hungarian aboard? We need an interpreter—instantly!
"

It took them a second to come to life.

"Galli, the assistant pastry chef," said the doctor. "He knows Hungarian. I treat him for his sprain."

"Get him at once," the first officer barked. He was beginning to look drawn.

The doctor went to a wall phone and dialed. Klára's murmur of Hungarian went on, now a mumble, now shrill singsong.

"Klára, who did this to you?"

I asked it again when she paused for breath. "Speak English."

The first officer tried it in French. But all we got back was the language we did not understand, with *vezetö* frequently repeated. Finally she fell silent.

"Where in hell is that pastry chef?"

"He is coming to the phone, *m'sieu*. He was in his bunk."

"What will happen next about this?" I asked the first officer.

"There will be an investigation. It is clearly murder. I will so inform the captain."

I drew on my slender French. *"C'est fantastique."*

"Oui. C'est horrible."

"How long ago was she discovered?"

He looked at his wrist watch. "About thirty minutes."

I looked at mine. It was five past midnight.

We waited in silence. Klára began mumbling again, but more faintly now. A nurse came in, still buttoning the last button of her uniform, saw what lay on the operating table, blanched, and, at a gesture from the doctor, stood to one side.

The door opened again and a plump, elderly, bald man came in. "You sent for me?"

"She is speaking Hungarian," the first officer told him. "She is dying. Act quickly. Ask her who attacked her. At once."

The plump little man looked frightened. "Attacked her?"

"Hurry."

He turned to her. As he did, the mumble gurgled in her throat and stopped. The doctor moved fast to her.

"C'est fini," he said somberly. "She is dead."

Now all I had was what had sounded like *vegeta meg ult engine*. We all looked at each other and then we looked away. The awareness of death comes strangely. But it always comes, sooner or later.

The nurse brought a white sheet with which to cover her. I plucked the pastry chef's arm.

"What does this mean?" and I read what had sounded like *vegeta meg ult engine* as best I could. I repeated several versions, slowly. He looked puzzled.

"I think what you say," he said at last, "is 'I was killed by the lord.' Or 'the master.' It is hard to translate *vezetö*."

"Or the boss?"

"It could mean something like that, yes. Or 'He had me killed.'"

* * * *

The first officer hurried out to report to the captain, even as the nurse and the doctor began wheeling Klára's body out to wherever they store bodies on a ship. I was left alone, except for the pastry chef. He looked at me, shrugged, and went out slowly. Everyone seemed to have something to do.

I had something to do too, and the mere thought of it chilled me.

I went up to the little aft bar, which was virtually empty. I ordered a double cognac and I put it down fast, with malice aforethought. Sometimes malice aforethought makes a good chaser.

I waited for it to hit. And settle. And act. Then I went out on deck.

The last thing in the world I wanted was to be seen fooling around lifeboats, but I went to the one containing Jones's body. At least my knots, learned years ago as a Boy Scout, had held; the tarpaulin was still intact.

I stood in close to the cabin wall and looked up at the dark bridge. Anyone up there could look down and observe me—could be watching me right now. And I couldn't see him at all. It was a chance I'd have to take.

But I hesitated nervously for a moment, and looked around, and I saw the sea aft was oddly littered with clots of debris. Then I realized what it was. The kitchen crew was dumping garbage.

Now or never.

I walked to the lifeboat and fumbled the knots loose. Standing on tiptoe I looked into the boat. It was pitch dark.

I lit a match; the wind instantly blew it out. That was bad, for that little gleam could easily have been noticed from the bridge. I put the paper of matches into the boat and under the tarpaulin before lighting the next match. The instant it ignited, I dropped it inside the boat.

The match flared for only a second, but in that time I glimpsed Jones's face, the lips drawn back from the teeth in an animal snarl. *Rigor mortis.*

But anyway he was there, and he had not been discovered.

I retied the knots with shaking fingers and retreated into the lee of the cabin wall, hoping fervently I had not been seen. Between this and what the cold, precise Widow's-Peak Pennypacker could tell about me, I undoubtedly could be sent up for life, plus ten years.

When I returned to the grand salon, I stood at the doorway and saw that another officer had joined our table. Tom was saying something, and they all laughed at it. They were having fun. I looked at the captain's table. Merrilee was still there, glowing, and every officer's head was turned toward her.

She was having fun too.

The thing for me to do was get to work, and the work that most needed doing right now was to search her suite. But this was not the night to risk being caught snooping in Merrilee Moore's suite. So I went back to the table and said, "What's new?" and sat down.

Twit-Twit put her lips close to my ear. "What did that first officer want?"

"The captain lost his bearings. He wanted me to straighten him out."

The other officer, eavesdropping, chuckled. Obviously he had not heard the news yet.

But Twit-Twit looked at me, not suspiciously as I would have expected, but with a kind of sympathetic understanding, even though she knew nothing about what was going on.

You'd almost think she was intuitive. Or psychic.

CHAPTER 13

Porthole

I awoke early and slowly, gradually discovering that I was feeling a little less than well. I had succumbed last night, or, to be exact, about five hours before I awoke, to the various pressures afflicting me. To be more exact, I had worked my way much farther into the cognac. Now, at a little after 9 a.m., I was beginning to work my way out. It would take a while.

There was a vague sound, or something that sounded like a sound. It repeated and now was a definite bang. Someone was prowling around the suite. I swung out of bed quietly, and Tom's voice spoke in ominous tones.

"Sorry. I'm one of those things that go bump in the night. Did I wake you?"

"No. What are you up to?"

"I don't know. It must be that God-damn champagne."

"Personally, I blame the God-damn brandy."

"Why do women force men to drink against our wills?"

I took a pull at the ice water direct out of the carafe.

"What are you up to? As I seem to remember someone saying earlier. Myself, I guess."

"I don't know. I'm either going to get dressed, or else I am going back to bed. Or maybe I'm going to have a little hair of the dog. Or maybe all three."

Memory came flooding back in waves, of yesterday and last night, and each wave was taller and more overwhelming than the last.

"I'll go along with you and take all three, doubled. Let's go."

"The drink first?"

"I'll wait a while. You go ahead."

"Maybe I will." He thumbed the cork out of the bottle still resting in the champagne bucket. "Still cold," he said, poured, sipped, drank, sighed grate-fully. "Damned good thing I don't *really* like champagne."

"Damned good."

I went in and took a long shower.

When I came out, it was a couple of glasses of champagne later. I felt better and so did Tom.

He said, "You know what? I think I'll put on some underwear. Just as a start. Just to see what it will feel like."

"Everything generally okay?"

"More or less. Less, I guess."

"Two will get you five I feel worse than you do."

"Why should you? What right do you have?"

"I won't go into it now. Maybe at lunch."

And maybe I would. I'd done some thinking in the shower. "I'm going to shave." I did, to the accompaniment of an occasional gurgle in the other room. No one hates champagne like Tom Dolan.

When all the lather was scraped off and I hadn't cut myself, I said, "I see myself again. In the mirror." I suppose I was a little lightheaded. "I look the same."

"Why shouldn't you?"

"Every day it's the same face. I don't change. It's discouraging."

"Have some wine."

"No. Onion soup."

"That's a great idea. A hell of a great idea. The French Line. God bless it. Onion soup for breakfast."

"Then get dressed."

"No. It's not *that* great an idea. If you see the steward, order me some, to be brought in at 11 a.m." He moved toward his cabin with the champagne bottle.

"Where are you going?"

"A man must have his rest." He waved the bottle. "Back to bed."

Betsy's voice called, "Tom, what are you doing?"

Tom took one more long draught from the bottle and put it down outside their door. "Coming, mother. See you later, man." He went in.

I got dressed. I had a bug to find, and I had a little plan.

* * * *

When I knocked at the door of B-78 I did not get an immediate answer. I did not expect one. She had no maid now, and she undoubtedly was dead-tired, and she'd probably taken a sleeping pill as well. So I knocked again presently, and louder, and got no response.

I knocked a third time.

Was she there at all? She must be. Where could she, of all people, have gone at only ten minutes after ten?

I walked out on deck and around to her windows and peered in. If some-one saw me, I was a Peeping Tom, trying to look in on the most glamorous woman in the world as she lay in bed, presumably naked, since that was the widely advertised way she was supposed to sleep.

But as nearly as I could see through a half-lowered Venetian blind, the bed had been turned down for sleeping, but no one was in it, and no one had been.

I knocked on the window and, as I did, I scanned the light-beige carpet in the cabin for bloodstains, remembering the maid. There was no sign of struggle or disorder. I walked back through the corridor companionway and quietly tried the doorknob. It was locked. I began, just slightly, to worry. For I thought of the garbage-dumping earlier. She was concerned about people falling overboard. If she had seen something go over the side, or float away in the ship's wake...

Hell with that. She could not be that impulsive.

But I began looking around the ship, looking in the public rooms to see if by any chance she had gotten up early and decided to have a massage in the health room (which was closed tight), or a swim in the pool (no; she had said she didn't swim), or write some letters (the library was empty).

But the only person I met was Dr. Cyclops, the man with the bad eye, who brushed past, and when I looked in the dining salon it was almost empty. Onion soup did not seem attractive. I was worried.

But as I made the rounds of the decks, I kept an eye peeled for bloodstains. Klára had been struck down and bloodily beaten *someplace*. Where? It could be findable.

I saw no bloodstains anywhere. As I walked past our own suite the big steak-lover, who roomed next to us and ate at Cotton-Hair Pennypacker's table, was complaining again to our patient-looking steward.

"What do you mean, no Westphalian?" he was demanding. "It is always on the menu."

"But the *machina, m'sieu*," the steward said. His knuckles, held stiffly at his side, were white.

"The *what*?"

"The *machina*. Machine that slices. The kitchen cannot slice the ham."

"Why not?"

"The machine is gone. They are—how you say?—search for it."

"That's ridiculous. You can't lose a meat slicer. Anyway, they can slice it by hand."

I continued my tour of the ship. I did not see Merrilee.

So I finally went back to her cabin. Maybe she had gone for a stroll on the deck, and I just happened to have missed her.

But as I approached the door a maid came along, and then another, and they both looked at me.

"Is Miss Moore up, do you happen to know?"

They looked at each other and one of them said something in French which I did not understand.

"I don't know, *m'sieu*," said the other. "She was not a few moments ago. I looked in, quietly."

"Her personal maid—she had an accident last night."

"We know about it, *m'sieu*."

The other one said something else in French, and looked alarmed saying it.

On a sort of crazy impulse, I spoke peremptorily. "What did she say?"

They looked at each other with dismay.

"What did you say?" I repeated harshly.

"She—she say, there was a fight. Between *Mademoiselle* Moore. And her maid. The dead woman."

"When was this?"

"Last night. When *Mademoiselle* Moore dresses."

"What kind of a fight?"

"That maid. She is an evil woman."

"She's a dead woman."

"*Oui*. But Michele here say she argue *Mademoiselle* Moore to go back to United States. Right away. When land *en Angleterre*. And *la mademoiselle* refuse. So they argue. So that maid—her name—"

"Klára."

"*Une* Hungarian. An evil woman. She argue hard with the *mademoiselle*. She shout, get mad and scream. Michele heard. She was doing the bathroom."

"Okay. *Merci*."

I pulled two dollar bills from my pocket. "When *Mademoiselle* Moore returns, tell her to call me on the telephone, please. Here is the number." I scrawled the suite number on one of the bills and gave it to her. She looked pleased.

I don't know how I looked myself, but anxious is probably accurate.

* * * *

I went back to the suite and let myself in. I didn't feel like breakfast.

Tom's bottle of champagne was still by the closed door to their state-room, Twit-Twit's door was not quite shut. I went to it and looked in. She was sound asleep, huddled under a mound of blankets in the bed, while cold sea air poured in the window. She looked like a tousle-haired ten-year-old.

I closed the door softly.

The phone rang and I leaped to it.

"Hello? Mr. Deacon?" The voice had a familiar huskiness. "Where the hell have you been?"

I heard a kind of hoarse giggle. Was she tight?

"Guess where I am. Right now."

"Where are you?"

"I'm in Sam's stateroom."

"Is that where you've been all this time?"

"Never mind. Look. I've discovered something."

"What is it?"

"Remember? We won't talk on the phone. But it's something heavy and it should be taken out of this stateroom. Now here's what you should do."

The low husky voice had an urgency.

"I'll pass it to you out of the porthole. When you see it, you'll realize why I'm being careful. Now do this. Right away. Walk along the outer deck, alongside Sam's stateroom. That's the main deck. It's the fourth porthole on the starboard side—that's the right side, right?"

"Check."

"Wait until no one is in sight, then just reach in and take what I will give you. Put it under your coat and walk away. Then I'll call you."

"You're in the stateroom now?"

"Yes. And I'd better not stay here much longer. Walk up to the porthole whistling a little, so I'll know. Then reach in."

"Right."

"I'll have the porthole all unscrewed and open."

"Go ahead. Two minutes from now."

I moved fast, found my way down the several staircases to "A" deck and went out into the weather. The ship was plunging deeply, and the spray came sudden as a whip across your face.

There was no one on the starboard side of "A" deck. That was fine. I located the fourth porthole and walked past it. It was open.

I turned around, walked toward it, and began whistling. Still no one was coming, either way. So I continued whistling—"High Society," which is basically a march—and thus I marched up to the porthole. I put my hand up to it. What had she found?

Even as I reached in, everything fit together. Maybe it's because I heard a low humming. But there flashed through my mind the memory of trying, years ago, to unscrew the big wing-nuts on a porthole. I thought of Merrilee's pretty but slender fingers. I thought—

My arm was in, hand open and waiting for her to put into it whatever she was going to give me.

And I pulled my hand out as the humming sound suddenly rose. I glimpsed a whirling, shiny steel blade where my hand had been, saw it rise and move quickly across the porthole. And vanish.

It was an electric meat slicer. It had almost cut off my right hand. That was why our stateroom neighbor, a little earlier, could not get his Westphalian.

What do you do when something like that happens? Do you know? I can tell you. You get a little sick and scared and numb for a moment, and walk away fast.

Then sanity and anger return, and you walk faster toward the son of a bitch who tried to maim you. At least, that is what I did. Suddenly I was ready to kill.

At Sad Sam Jones's cabin, I hit the door with my shoulder; it flew open. The meat sheer lay sidewise on the floor, the razor-like circular blade still spinning and detached from the heavy steel platen it usually stood on.

But the room was empty. So, I discovered in a few strides, were the bath and closet.

No Merrilee. No anyone.

As I looked around, sanity returned, and I began to understand what they had tried to do. They hadn't wanted to kill me; it wasn't that important. They just wanted to make me an object lesson to her. Me now. Her later. That was the object lesson.

And where was *she?*

I looked down at my right hand. It was still there. So were all the fingers. For that I could thank my slow, somewhat hung-over, reflexes.

Near the slicing machine's platen lay a small tube that could have been toothpaste. I picked it up. It was theatrical make-up—green grease paint. It was a familiar shade of green. I had seen it before, and I could see it again— on my severed hand.

Suddenly I felt sick. I had to go into the bathroom, where I stood over the toilet without really up-chucking. I stood there, cold and shaken.

This took a little while.

Then I picked up the circular-blade part, yanked its cord out of the wall, and left without trying to conceal anything. I found my way to Widow's-Peak Pennypacker's cabin, put it down in front of the door, and left.

On my way to our suite, I passed the guy with the mesh gloves. He apparently had just come out of his stateroom, for he looked sleepy and was smoothing his gloves on; and he looked at me without seeing me. He was walking fast. I wondered what language he spoke.

In the suite, I took off my jacket and shirt, debated Tom's wine bottle and decided against it, and Twit-Twit emerged from her room.

"Where did you go?"

"Out. A walk around the promenade deck."

I pulled her over to the bed, kicked off my loafers, lay down, settled her beside me, and said, "Shut up."

As I've said, Twit-Twit sometimes seems psychic. She just lay there, and I kept my arm around her and enjoyed the comfort of her warm, slender waist and of sensing that she knew how I felt without knowing why I felt that way.

After a while we both dozed, or semi-dozed, but I didn't really sleep. We didn't do anything else, either.

We understood something unspoken between us.

CHAPTER 14

The Note and the Cable

Across the pool, one of the bundled-up college girls was playing a guitar. Another was beating a shining spoon in her bouillon cup, and the rest were clapping their hands and chanting something that sounded like a cross between folk music and a mazurka by Bartok. Everyone was sitting blanketed in deck chairs, smiling at them, and even enjoying the cold, sullen sky and wet North Atlantic air. And relaxing.

I was trying to relax. And making progress because I'd come to a decision a while before, and was only waiting for the opportune moment to put it into effect. Betsy was lying back, eyes closed, in her new deck chair—new because the first had turned up missing somehow, although of course her name was on it. Someone else had taken it and the steward had brought another. Twit-Twit was brushing up on her French with a volume of Malraux, Tom was dozing, probably with the help of the champagne.

Where my charge was, I did not know, but it had occurred to me that the captain and others must have wanted to break the news and then question her about the death of the maid.

The problem was solved by the deck steward, who came up with an envelope on a tray and touched his cap.

I thumbed the envelope open. The scrawl inside said:

"I'm sort of lonesome. Can I have lunch at your table?"

I took the steward's pencil and wrote:

"Of course. One o'clock at the smoking room bar first. Where have you been?"

I handed it back to him.

"Where did you get this?"

"Mademoiselle Moore. In her room, *m'sieu.* She gave it to me."

"Personally?"

"Personally, *m'sieu.*" His eyes lit up. He'd seen her all right. "A moment ago."

I said, "Fine. Tell her to stay there," and tipped him, although it wasn't necessary, but just to make sure he would deliver the message.

I felt lighthearted.

"Fan mail?" asked Tom.

"Another autograph hound. You know how it is."

"Who was it, really?" said Twit-Twit.

This was as good a time as any.

So I told them the whole story of Merrilee's fears, and Kane and Compton and the two murders, and what I was up to, and how they happened to be aboard. It took some time.

Then Twit-Twit said, "Do you really think she has ESP powers?"

"I doubt it, on the basis of present evidence. That business about the falling ceiling and the red skirt might well be coincidence. But her mother may have been another cup of tea. If the mother did show occasional flashes of supranormal gifts, it might well have made Merrilee think she herself had some too. And it would certainly lend a lot of weight to her mother's prophecy about crossing the ocean."

"You think someone's really after her," Tom said.

"I know it."

"Who?"

A tall, dark-haired woman in a flame-colored coat dropped into the deck chair next to me. It was the chair that Merrilee had occupied yesterday, but had no name on it. Because of the weather, not too many people had taken deck chairs.

"Mawnin'," she said to me, or to no one in particular, in a southern sorghum accent you could have cut with a cookie cutter.

"Good morning."

"It's bettuh than last ni-yut," she said.

I recognized her. She looked younger and prettier and more natural than she had when she first came aboard with the college girls. She was their chaperone.

She smiled, curled up in a blanket, closed her eyes, and, as far as I could tell, went instantly to sleep.

I went back to what Tom had asked, leaned over to them, and spoke in a low voice. "I don't know who. But I can tell you who are on board and I think look screwy. Or odd. There's this guy Pennypacker."

"The old man with the white hair who wants to play bridge?" asked Betsy, awed.

"The other one. Although, maybe—but there are others."

"Like who?"

"There's an old Indian who's always around. And a joker with a bad eye who seems interested in my phone calls."

Oddly, I thought of the girl who had just sat down near me and was presumably sound asleep. But I turned my back on her to make sure she couldn't near my low mumble. That's what suspicion does for you.

No one said anything for a while. "If I were going to try to do what you have suggested is being done to your—your girlfriend," said Tom, "I'd think about the ship's personnel."

"Yes. Maybe. Like who?"

"Like a steward. Or maid."

"Or an officer?"

"Yes. Maybe. As you like to say."

"How much is really at stake?" said Twit-Twit.

"The picture is worth at least twenty-five million dollars, if it turns out to be worth anything, and quite possibly triple that if it comes off. Think of *Gone With the Wind*."

A brightly buttoned page came up to me.

"*M'sieu* Deacon? There is a message for you in the radio room."

"I'm impressed," said Betsy.

"Another phone call," I said.

"Not a telephone, *m'sieu*," the steward said. "A cable. They tried to deliver it to your room."

Tom got up too. "Then deliver it to him in the bar," he said. "The aft bar. If it's bad news that's the best place to receive it."

"You're right. Also if it's good news."

"The aft bar, *m'sieu*?" said the steward uncertainly.

"Well, maybe it's sort of half-aft," said Tom, and led the way before his wife could reprimand him.

As we walked down the deck, we saw our deck steward bending over two blanketed figures.

"But these are not your chairs, *m'sieu*," he was saying.

"Whose are they, for Chris'sake?" demanded a familiar voice, and I recognized our neighbor, the steak-lover.

"*Le nom c'est sur la carte, m'sieu.*"

"Say it in English!"

"Be'ind you."

He twisted around in the chair. "Mrs. Dolan! Who the hell is that?"

Tom and I swung around. The mystery of Betsy's missing deck chair was solved.

The steward began, "*M'sieu* the chairs are rented. There is *une carte*—a card, telling the name of whom 'as the chair."

Tom moved the steward out of the way, gently. "Mrs. Dolan happens to be my wife," he said sweetly. "You obviously stole her chair. So suppose you obviously return it, with an apology. Right now. The steward will show you where to carry it. And if you don't, I'm going to beat you up when I come back, and throw you in the sea. As you may notice, I'm saying it in English."

We went on to the bar.

"I shouldn't lose my temper like that."

"I thought you did well."

"A Martini?"

"A Martini."

The boy brought the little tissue-paper envelope containing the cable just as the drinks were placed in front of us. I sipped a cold clean dryness, slit the envelope, and read the message. It was terse and meaningful:

> Five nine and half. Hundred fifty eight pounds. Forty seven. Lean build. Brown and brown, little gray. Thin face, widow's peak, mastoid scar left, scraggly teeth. Careful dresser, mother's wedding ring on left hand always. Probably fag. Carries. Love, doll.

I read it twice and passed it over to Tom. Madelyn had done well. That was the second Pennypacker to the teeth—literally. He was the industrial spy.

Tom said, "An identification, I take it."

"Of the guy whose cabin I tried to prowl. He's the spy, all right."

"One word I don't get. 'Carries.'"

"A weapon. Underworld lingo. It means he packs a gun all the time."

"That's nice." He studied the cable. "'Love doll,' eh? I won't ask who that is."

"It's from a researcher at the office named Madelyn who looked all this up for me. You just didn't read it right. If you had, you'd see it's love *comma* doll. In other words, she's sending me love."

"And she's calling you doll."

"Why the hell not?"

"She's calling you comma doll, actually. Mama doll and comma doll."

"That's pretty funny. Who writes your material?"

"Bob Hope."

"Bob Hope and Gordon's gin. I think the gin works faster. Actually, she's a hell of a nice girl."

"From where I sit you know nothing but nice girls. Does Merrilee have a friend?"

He waved for two more drinks and thought a little while. Finally he spoke in a low voice, almost out of the side of his mouth. There were others at the bar now.

"Where I sit, you're into something kind of deep."

"From where I sit, too."

"You think this Pennypacker is the guy? I mean who killed these two people?"

"I don't know that much yet. I now know for sure that he is who I suspected he was. But I have never known of his doing any killing at all. And two deaths on one job is kind of a lot."

"Maybe he has an assistant."

"That's an idea. The share-the-work principle. And, of course, there's always the possibility that Roger Kane, the producer, is himself aboard and doing the dirty work. But Newt, at least, doesn't think so. He feels that Kane would engineer just about anything but that he'd delegate the actual work to someone else."

"What the hell are you going to do about it?"

"Check some alibis. We know more or less how the maid died and when. The press agent hasn't been found yet, but we can figure to a certain extent on the time of his killing. Moving that body into the suite and rigging it up took time, certainly. The killer must be wondering where it is."

"It's a real dance-in-the-dark."

"Sure. But if I can find out who was where at the time each of these people was killed—"

"What do you mean by *who*?"

"As I said, there are quite a few people I wonder about."

"Like?"

"I mentioned the Indian and the man with the bad eye. Then there's an odd-ball who wears gloves all the time and escorts a kind of harem queen. Sat near us last night."

"I remember."

"Who else? Maybe the other Pennypacker—Old Granddad. That coincidence of names—well, may be just coincidence. Or as you said, a ship's officer. There's really enough at stake to justify bribing all kinds of people."

"Drink your drink," said Tom. "I think you're getting hysterical." Then, getting up, "You'll need help checking those alibis."

As we passed a table where people were having drinks before lunch, I heard a woman say, "Our steward tells us absolutely it was Merrilee Moore's maid, and that they had been fighting like mad. Merrilee had fired her for stealing or something."

* * * *

"What number did you pick today?" Betsy asked as we walked up to the deck chairs.

Tom shook his head. "I'm busy today. No time to dope hunches. And besides, I don't feel lucky."

Betsy got up. "Well, I do. I just got my right chair back, not that it mattered. From some rather nasty, mumbling man. But I'm going down and play the pool again. Come on." She took his arm.

I dropped down into the chair and pulled the blanket up.

"Big morning?" asked Twit-Twit.

"Fairly big."

"You're getting to be quite the detective."

"I'm no detective."

"You do fairly well. Or is it just the clients that attract you?"

"Stop it. If you think there's anything between me and Merrilee, you're nutty as a fruitcake. You know who really mixed me up in this? You, you clothes-crazy bitch. You wanted to go to Paris."

She laughed, a gay little laugh, and she can laugh nastily when she feels like it.

"I know. I found out your intentions quite early."

"What does that mean?"

"You said that when you first met Merrilee on the boat deck you thought someone was spying on you."

"I still think so."

"You're right."

"Who?"

"I can play detective, too."

"You?"

"You can't get away from me that easily, Beady-eyes."

I patted her under the blanket. "I've never wanted to. But how did you know where to be?"

"The steward came to the suite that evening, when you were out."

"Yes."

"He asked if you had received your message all right, because he had been told to slip it under the door. I said I guessed you had. But I wondered. Then I saw a little balled-up piece of paper in the wastebasket, and I read it. So I just took a stroll at the appointed time."

"Okay, detective."

"Mind if I say something else?"

I patted again for an answer.

"Speaking of suspects, how about Merrilee? It was her maid and her press agent."

"Yes. But I don't think so."

"Had you considered her at all?"

"To tell the truth, no. After all, as we private eyes say, she's the client."

"And she *is* attractive."

"Bitch!"

CHAPTER 15

A Little Further Knowledge of the Score

But after establishing Twit-Twit at the bar with the Dolans, I left and went to the library. I got out the *Who's Who* and this time read all there was to read about the other Pennypacker that the book listed.

Besides being a retired professor of psychology, he had been born in Long Beach sixty-four years ago, I learned, had married Edith Sweet, was evidently childless, had an M.A from Ohio State University, a Viennese doctorate, and had published in professional journals: "The Psychic Bases of Sadism," "Compulsive Transvestitism," "Detecting Pathological Lying, So-Called." He was associated with a psychological testing laboratory and his home was in Long Beach.

I went back to the bar, so thoughtfully that for a time I ignored my drink, and Merrilee even slipped onto the bar stool next to me without my immediately knowing she was there. A lot of other people did, though; every eye in the place was on her.

I performed introductions, and it was nice to notice how everyone accepted everyone without the self-conscious effluvia that often accompanies the introduction of a celebrity. She said she'd have a Dubonnet on the rocks, and the bartender practically sprinted for the bottle. She looked palely in need of it.

When I got a chance I said *sotto voce*, "Are you all right?"

"Of course. I guess. I don't know. I've—I've been crying. Klára was... was...I don't have any real friends, you know. She—I depended on her. And I have no one now."

"Yes, you do. Drink your drink."

She barely sipped it. "Drinks don't help. When you're really alone."

"Where *were* you this morning?"

"In my cabin."

"Like hell you were. I dropped by, knocked several times, and the maid went in. She said your bed hadn't been slept in."

"The maid was right. I slept in the tub."

"The tub!"

"Yes. I got in awfully late from the party, and Klára wasn't—that's why I wanted to have lunch with you. Because I feel so *alone*. I don't know anyone on the ship, really. I hope your friends don't mind too much."

"Don't be silly. They'll love you."

She gave me a sudden child-smile of appreciation. She wanted to be loved, and she needed to be. It was so ironic. She needed plain, simple affection far more than the average, plain, simple girl.

She went on. "When I got in last night I didn't know about Klára, of course. It was nice, their keeping it from me. I guess. But I couldn't sleep, and she wasn't there, so I finally drew a bath myself and got into the tub and let the warm water run slowly. It's a way I have of getting to sleep. Just lie in the tub with the warm water running slowly. Try it some time."

"I will."

"You probably don't have trouble getting to sleep. You look like that. You're lucky."

"Yes. So that's where you were this morning?"

"Until almost ten. Then I woke up. A little waterlogged. Someone was pounding on my door."

"One of the officers?"

"Two of them. They—they broke the news. And then took me to the captain, who wanted to ask me some questions. They were all really very nice. Sympathetic. Everyone has been so nice."

"I'm sure they were." Twit-Twit, next to me, was listening with more than half an ear. I leaned back to include her in the conversation; after all, I didn't want another civil war. "They wanted to know when you last saw Klára, no doubt."

"Yes."

"When did you?"

"I can't bear to think about it. When I left my stateroom to go to the party, about ten-thirty. We'd been—been arguing."

"What about?"

"Oh, she meant well, poor thing. But she began giving me this hard sell again about going back to New York as soon as we landed. I finally had to shut her up. I hate myself now."

"How could you know what would happen? What else did they ask you?"

"Where I was before and around midnight."

That was about when she and I had gone for a walk on the deck. Who were they checking on, her or me?

"Why? That's when they figure Klára was attacked."

"Yes. It has something to do with the blood coagu—you know what I mean. Anyway, the doctor figures it happened between 11 and 11:30."

I began trying to remember who had been in the salon at that particular time. Everybody, it seemed. Mesh-Gloves for sure, although exactly when he had come in I was not sure. The first officer, yes. Widow's-Peak Pennypacker? I thought he was. With the college girls. I couldn't remember. Old Cotton-Hair Pennypacker? No, definitely. The Indian? Dr. Cyclops? I couldn't remember. Maybe Tom could.

"How about lunch?" Betsy was saying. "Lunch anyone? I'm starved."

"So am I," I said. Merrilee had hardly touched her drink. "What do you say, Twit?"

"I'm for *le dejeuner*."

We went down for what I figured would be a restful and restorative lunch. And I was right—for a while.

* * * *

The steak-lover was not complaining this noon, and Cotton-Hair Pennypacker looked over and waved but did not ask us to play bridge. Maybe the fifth person at our table overwhelmed him. Widow's-Peak Pennypacker ate by himself as usual, tasting the cold salmon and its accompanying mayonnaise intently. The Indian was there and so were the college girls and their tall, pretty chaperone. The murder, news of which must by now have spread all over the ship, did not seem to have disquieted anyone, nor was there noticeable talk of it. Especially at our table.

Tom read the ship's newspaper.

"I just want to see what the market did yesterday," he said.

"We're in the market," said Betsy. "We have A.T.&T. One share. We also have one share of I.B.M. Or is it B.M.I., dear?"

"B.M.I is an association of song writers, you mutton," said Tom.

"Then that's what we've got," said Betsy. "We'd never have anything valuable like I.B.M."

"Shut up," Tom growled cheerfully. At that moment the first officer came up to the table, cap in hand. He bowed to all of us. But he addressed Merrilee.

"*Pardon.* I 'ave been asked to give you this, *Mademoiselle.*"

It was a stateroom key.

"It is the key to your stateroom. It was in the apron pocket of the—of your maid. It is all she 'ad on her at the time in the way of the possessions."

"Oh." There was something poignant about that tagged rod of heavy brass. "Thank you." She put it on the table, as if she didn't like holding it.

He bowed all around again and left. I watched him go out, cap in hand, and observed how many other people were watching, too. Being with her a couple of hours was really moving into a goldfish bowl.

Tom was looking around at the others, too, and his gaze stopped at Widow's-Peak Pennypacker.

"I'd still like to get that guy for a TV interview," he said. "Next fall. If he'd open up."

"Maybe you could persuade him."

"Maybe I could if I asked him over here. He's sure interested in what's been going on at this table. I noticed it when the officer was standing here."

"Why don't you brace him after a while? Maybe he'd go for it."

"Maybe. You never can tell."

"Also, you might just find out where he was last night between 10:30 and midnight. I don't know that he was at the big gala all that time."

Tom looked at me. "Is that the time, and what we want to know?"

"That's what we want to know. About a lot of people."

"Then I brace. Tom Dolan, boy detective."

We had reached the coffee stage. Merrilee's fingers stroked the key.

"Why do you want to know that?" she asked.

"I just like to know things. Sometimes a couple of them fit together and tell me something more."

"Like what?"

I didn't want to go any further.

"Come on, Sherlock," said Twit-Twit. "Give us a f'r-instance."

"Well. Like that key."

"What more does that tell you?"

"That the people who killed Klára don't need it. Otherwise they wouldn't have left it in her apron. So it means they can get into your cabin any time they want without it. It's something to bear in mind, Merrilee. I'm serious."

"And with that happy thought," said Twit-Twit, pushing her chair back, "we'll leave you. Have your port and cigars, gentlemen. The ladies are retiring to the drawing room. Or to a stroll on deck. Why don't you come along, Merrilee?"

She got up, and had to balance herself against the ship's roll. Merrilee looked appealingly at me for an instant. "Will you drop by and see me in an hour?"

"Of course."

"I have—premonitions. Or something—you know what I mean. They have nothing to do with the key."

"Right. Forget about the key for now."

As a matter of fact, she did. She got up from the table and left the key where it was. Whatever else she was, she was irresponsible, and dependent on other people to pick up the pieces. And right now in a kind of daze.

Tom said, "More coffee?"

"Just a touch. I shouldn't have said that, I guess."

"Yes, you should have. It's a very valid point. She should be on her guard. And something should be done, like changing the lock."

"Something will be. I'll see to it."

Cotton-Hair Pennypacker, his wife, and the Steak-Lovers were getting up. He smiled at us as usual. "Got a little game going," he said. "Nothing else to do on an afternoon like this but play cards and forget the rolling."

"Right," said Tom.

"I've given up inviting you boys to play, at least temporarily." He grinned. "Our friends here—" he gestured toward the Steak-Lovers "—are joining Mrs. Pennypacker and me this afternoon. But I'll be after you again."

"And we're pretty scared about playing them," said Mrs. Steak-Lover.

"How is that?" I asked.

"You know how these business experts are. They're awful tricky." She smiled archly.

"Business expert?"

"Doctor Pennypacker is professor of business administration at Grinnell University," Steak-Lover announced importantly.

They got up.

"Well, don't take any wooden market-predictions," Tom said. "How are the chickadees?"

Pennypacker grinned. "Haven't a single stock to my name," he said. "And all five are great."

When they had left Tom said, "Let's get on with the war. Or the alibis. I'll talk to that other Pennypacker guy. Who else should I take?"

"Thanks. I'll take the guy with the bad eye—Dr. Cyclops, let's call him 'til I get his name. You take the little joker with the white-mesh gloves. He was eyeing Merrilee pretty closely last night. I'll take the Indian—and the first officer, because I have to talk to him anyway. He's supposed to be on our side."

"Do you really think he's a suspect?"

"All I have for sure is that two people have been killed, and the approximate time of each murder. If we find someone who has no real alibi for one, we begin to check that person on the time of the other. And we also know this—that the enemy is aboard, and he is probably a man, but he may have a girl assistant."

"We know all that? How?"

"I think the voice that lured me to Jones's porthole was a woman, trying to sound like Merrilee, though I could be wrong. But the maid was slugged by a man. It took strength to make those skull depressions."

"It might have been a woman in a maniacal fury."

"These are not crimes of passion. And if the killer is a man, it would make sense to give him a girl assistant, because a woman can do things and get places men cannot."

"Like girls' powder rooms."

"Exactly, Watson. Which reminds me—I'm latching onto that key." I dropped it in my pocket.

Tom was making little notes on his ship's newspaper. "Those crazy Mets," he said.

"What about them?"

"They won the opener yesterday. In thirteen innings. But did you ever see such a wild score?"

Somehow I knew what was coming, and I didn't want it to come.

"Look." His finger pointed to a line in the mimeographed sheet.

Mets 21 dodgers 19

I felt the normal air go out of my lungs and cold night vapor seep in.

"What the hell," said Tom. "You're white as a sheet."

CHAPTER 16

Strip, Tease, and Bug

I took a few turns around the promenade deck. There were not many people about.

The sea was a sullen undulation, cresting into whitecaps that seemed almost to snap their heads off, and occasionally a wave hurled itself so high it struck against the stout glass of the deck's forward enclosure. I had never felt a major ship so completely subdued by the ocean. It was like being an actor standing in the middle of a set designed for some 1890's melodrama.

How had that crazy prediction come true? I began to think how.

There was one way. It was a wild guess, but it could explain things.

And I could test it out.

* * * *

In the main-deck foyer I found a framed map of the ship and located the printshop, which was three decks below.

I found my way there by degrees. The door, which was decorated with a large metal box to receive copy or communications, was open wide, and a man in sweaty shirtsleeves was hand-setting type, his fingers deeply ink-stained. A stack of colorful dinner menus, the inner sides all blank at the moment, awaited the imprint that would tell the first-class passengers what triumphs the chefs had prepared for them that night.

"*Pardon* ," I said.

"*Oui, m'sieu.*"

"There was a baseball score in the paper this morning. An American baseball score. You know what I mean?"

"*Oui, m'sieu.*"

He looked longingly at the work he still had to do.

"Where did it come from?"

"From the radio, *m'sieu.* The radio office. They take all the news from New York. Or Le Havre. Depending on where is the ship."

"This was the Mets-and-Dodgers baseball game. It was a strange score."

"*Oui, m'sieu.*" He was being polite but he wanted to get rid of me.

"And that was the score that came in by radio? There is no chance of error?"

"*M'sieu,* I do the paper. Also the menus. Also the announcements. I do it all. I am busy, *m'sieu.* But I do not make many mistakes."

"And no one could have changed that score?"

For the first time he began looking at me with a certain respectful suspicion. He said, "*M'sieu,* I get the what-you-call copy from the radio. It is short. Brief. You know. I write it out longer and the officer goes over it. He—what you say?—edits it. Then I mimeograph it."

"And that's what happened last night?"

"*Oui, m'sieu.*"

"Who's the officer who does this?"

"Often the first officer, *m'sieu.* Because of the big party last night, the assistant purser took care of it. But he made no changes at all."

I said thanks very much.

Going to Merrilee's stateroom, I began wishing I had never left New York, or met Newton Harlow III.

I still couldn't believe it. But there it was.

* * * *

I knocked at her door and got no response. I waited a while and knocked louder. No one home. They were all still walking the enclosed deck. Good. I had a key in my pocket and a search to conduct.

I used the key, let myself into her suite, and closed the door softly. Then I threw the bolt, so I could not be easily interrupted by any of the help, and began a leisurely inspection of Merrilee's digs, even before starting to hunt the one thing that I wanted to make sure was either there or was not.

Besides the living room, with its good-sized closet, there was a bedroom with another closet, and the bathroom. How would you bug a place like that?

Hardly the bedroom. This was not a divorce case.

But where in the living room? Chandeliers were a great place, but there was no chandelier. Behind a picture? There were some, but they were screwed into place on the wall, and an inspection of the screws' painted heads told me none had been recently taken out and put back.

Somewhere around the baseboards? I started a circuit of the rooms. I'd gotten to the bedroom when I heard a scratching in the living room. It seemed to come from the outside door. But it didn't come again. A passer-by, perhaps, who happened to run his hand or key against the door.

It rasped again, and I saw the doorknob turn slowly, then turn back slowly. There came the surreptitious sound of a key sliding into the lock.

Nothing happened.

I knew what that could be. The man outside looking down the corridor each way. Then sliding the key in. Then another look each way to see if anyone was watching.

The lock made a loud, quick switching sound, and I leaped back into the bedroom. Someone was coming in.

There was only one place in the bedroom to hide; you couldn't get under that low-built bunk unless you were a thin suitcase. I strode into the closet, backed in among sheer, scented dresses and more intimate things, and pulled the door almost shut.

The outer door opened and closed with a positive click. Then the bolt was shot. Like myself, whoever had come in didn't want to be interrupted. I waited.

I listened.

I heard nothing. Then he came into the bedroom, moving quietly, and I heard the soft, uncertain sound of cloth being moved.

I was hunched over, leaning away from all the clothes hung behind me. After a while my back began to hurt and I wanted to move, but I didn't dare, for fear of knocking something off a hanger. I heard occasional undistinguishable sounds from beyond the door, and soft scufflings. That was all.

I had to look out. My fingers found the surface of the door. I pushed gently, and a crack opened up wide enough to let me see half the room. I looked out.

Merrilee was standing in the middle of the floor. She had been undressing all this time. She had just kicked off her shoes and she was barefoot. In fact, all she had on was some sort of thin tight panties and, as I looked, she rolled these slowly down her thighs and stepped out of them, naked.

She did not look at all like an international sex symbol. She didn't even look sexy, but rather like a slight, adolescent girl with breasts considerably smaller than millions of people thought.

This is based on memory. At the moment, I was in something of a panic.

All I could think of was that I was a Peeping Tom—unintentionally, but nonetheless about to be caught in the act of spying on the world's most desirable woman in a completely private moment. If I had only looked out thirty seconds earlier, or if she had taken off only her dress—but she was in the buff. What did I do now?

She was studying herself in the mirror, confident of her solitude, looking first at her face and then raising her breasts with her hands, critically. It was not the moment to step out of a closet, clear your throat, and say, "Hello, there. How's every little thing?"

She stepped backward, dropped her hands, then walked forward toward the mirror. As she did that, she became less adolescently sexless, for her flesh was like sun-tanned jelly, and it quivered like jelly as she moved; she was naturally sinuous and soft.

But I also felt myself blushing in an agony of embarrassment. I like girls; they're my favorite sex. But I don't like to spy on them unintentionally in their intimate moments, and I could not bear the thought of being caught doing it.

I rapped my knuckles on the door. "I'm in here," I called out. "Don't be alarmed. I'm coming out with my eyes shut."

I closed my eyes and stumbled out into the room and stood there. "I can explain everything," I grinned stupidly.

There was no gasp or scream or indignant reproach, or anything that I had anticipated. There was a rather delicious gurgle of laughter. Slowly I opened my eyes. She stood before me, still nude, utterly unselfconscious, and smiling.

"Whatever were you doing in my closet?" she laughed. "Hunting for that bug you mentioned?"

She still made no move to put anything on. She enjoyed her nudity and the embarrassment it caused me. But my embarrassment began to abate.

"Yes. I—I had your extra key. I came in. When I heard you at the door, I thought it might be a prowler—honestly, I had no idea it was you or that you were undressing."

She laughed again and then with one finger gently pushed me aside. She went to the closet, thoughtfully considered several negligees, selected one, and slipped into it unhurriedly. She stepped into mules, fluffed out her hair, and smiled mischievously.

"My, but you can blush," she said. "Certainly you've seen girls without clothes on before."

I exhaled. "Go to hell. It was—just the—the Peeping Tom aspect of it that—"

"Any time you want to peep, you come right in and peep, Tom."

We laughed at each other, but for different reasons. She was amused. I was relieved.

But whatever else I had done by my awkwardness, I had broken the spell of shock which had gripped her all day.

"Okay," I said. "Speaking of keys, I'm going to get your locks changed. But meanwhile I want to keep yours, and I also want to give you a key to our suite. Here. I can get another. Any time you feel alone or frightened or want a friendly word, drop in."

"I will. I'll hide in your closet for a change. What time do *you* undress?"

"Now, come on. Let me up. As a matter of fact, I want to get to work. You sit still and smoke your cigarette."

I began once more to search the bedroom. I didn't know how big an object I was looking for, but I knew that these days bugs could be pretty small. Her bed was bolted to the floor, with the headboard flush against the wall; it was possible but not likely that the device was behind that. There was nothing under the bed but a small traveling bag, and that was empty. I felt around the mattress edges and the springs underneath. Nothing.

She smoked and watched.

The bathroom was tiled and barren. I probed the jars of cold cream and other things with a long pin, even though it seemed unlikely that the bug could be buried in one of them. I went through the clothes in the closet carefully and inspected the telephone on the night stand. Still nothing. Finally I felt and probed the chairs and their cushions, upended two little tables and the lamps. Nothing.

I went back to the living room, sat down, and thought a minute. She followed me, distractingly. The negligee was only moderately opaque.

I tried resolutely to put myself in the other fellow's place. The day bed, obviously. I took the pillows off it and felt each one. I pulled out the lower part to make it twin beds—and that's where I found it. I found more than I thought.

The gadget itself was a small black metal box, not much bigger than a match box, with a little round grill on each side suggesting a microphone. It was suspended from the springs of the lower part of the day bed, near the wall, where someone lying in bed could easily reach it. It could pick up sounds in the room, and someone in the bed could whisper into it.

The most interesting thing about it, however, was the little switch on the top, marked *On* and *Off*. Right now it was at the *Off* position. That was a good thing.

"Ever see this before?"

She took it from me with slightly shaky fingers.

"Why, no. What in the world *is* it?"

"It's what I've been looking for. The bug."

"So someone has been eavesdropping on me?"

"Oh, yes. With a little inside help." I pointed to the switch. "Someone had to turn that on and off at the right times."

"But who could do that?"

"It was concealed in your maid's bed."

"Not—oh, no! It couldn't have been Klára!"

"It had to be someone who was in the room a lot, and they could hardly depend on a steward or ship's maid to always be in at the right times."

"But Klára was as—as faithful as—"

"I'm afraid she wasn't. Didn't you tell me she was leaving you permanently on this trip and going home to Hungary for good? A few thousand bucks extra could have looked awfully good to her. It may also explain why she was killed."

"Why?"

"She obviously was working for *them*. She would go a certain way for them. Maybe she believed in your mother's ESP powers, or precognitive gift, or whatever you want to call it."

"She did."

"But when her persuasion about returning to New York did not work, it could well be that they wanted her to do something more, something more inimical to you, and that she refused. They couldn't afford to let it stop there. Killing her not only would silence her, but it would frighten you even more. Maybe they had another green-face act in mind and hid her body in the lifeboat only momentarily."

"Who's 'they'? You—you make them sound like an army."

"We know who the real 'they' is. He's presumably in California. He has representatives on the ship, though, and he expects them to produce results. The chances are he doesn't even know how they are going about it."

I thought a minute.

"You know, maybe you'll sleep in our suite tonight. In my bed."

"I will?"

She did not sound shocked.

"And I will sleep here—in your bed."

"What will that do?"

"It will make you safer. No one will know where you are. And someone may come calling here. With one or two little breaks in our favor, we could wrap this whole thing up tonight. Meanwhile—"

I hung the bug back on the bedsprings and pushed the two halves back into a day bed.

"It's off now. But each time you come in, just reach down like this—" I illustrated "—and feel the switch. If it's in the upper position, the bug is on, and you are being overheard. Don't let that scare you. Just behave normally. But don't say anything confidential to anyone. And don't turn the bug off, either. We don't want them to know we know it's there. That way we can use it against them. And we will."

"Gee whiz." Her eyes shone with excitement.

"Oh, there's one other thing. How much do you know about baseball?"

"Why—not much. Three strikes are out, and there's a pitcher's plate and so on."

"Mound. The plate is home. But do you follow baseball? Did you ever see a game?"

"Not a real game, no. I guess I really don't know much about it at all—as I suppose you gathered from the score I predicted yesterday. Did you ever hear what the real score was?"

"I'll check it when I get a chance."

She wrapped the negligee around herself a little more tightly. It was getting a little difficult to leave. "What was it you wanted to tell me?" I asked.

"Tell you?"

"You asked me to stop by and see you."

"Uh, yes." She smiled, and it was as if the sun had broken out over the stormy sea. "I guess I've forgotten now. Maybe I just wanted to talk to you." Lightning flashed from the brilliant sun. "I—sometimes I need, what do you call it? Reassurance."

"Now you have the key to it," I said. "But be careful who you let in here."

"I will."

"Also..." I hated to bring up something unpleasant. "Going back to Sam Jones. I saw him in the bar, the night before last, until one o'clock. You called me about six-thirty. He was dead then, in your closet, although you didn't know it, and he had been for some time. Did you hear from him at all after one o'clock?"

"No. As I said, I took a pill—"

"So you were asleep by when? One-thirty? At the latest?"

"About that."

"And Klára?"

"I think I heard her mattress creak before I went to sleep."

"And you called Jones about six-thirty."

"Earlier. It probably was nearer five-thirty the first time. I couldn't sleep. I don't know why. But I couldn't. I got no answer."

"And you stayed awake after five-thirty?"

"Yes. I called him again, a little after six. Still no answer. So I began to worry, and then I called you. But why is all this important?"

"I'm trying to figure out when he was killed. I'll say it was between one-thirty and two, yesterday morning. Because when I dragged him out of here, he was still wearing the same clothes that he had worn earlier in the bar. He somewhat needed a shave."

"He did?"

"And his bed had not been slept in. But most of all—" I wasn't sure of how much to go into.

"What?"

"His body had begun to stiffen at the time I dragged him out, even though it had been in a warm closet."

"Stop saying such awful things."

"Sorry. But you see what I mean. You had to go to sleep—and be fast asleep—before they could bring him in here, tie the rope, and all that. Which means they could not dare come in here to leave him earlier than two. At which time he was dead. So he was killed sometime after 1:00 a.m., but probably no later than two."

"Sometimes you say things that scare me."

"I don't mean to scare anyone. What are you going to do now?"

"I was going to bathe. I am uncomfortable if I don't bathe twice a day. Then your cute girlfriends and I are going to the afternoon movie. Then I get my hair done."

"Okay. See you later."

I started for the door. At least I thought I started for the door. She came forward.

"Just lock your door when I leave, and keep it locked. Be sure of who's there before you open it." Her eyes glistened wetly. "And remember. You'll be safe tonight in our suite." Somehow...anyhow...I anyway...put my awkward arms around her and held her for a time, and then I kissed her. Not one of those quick brother-and-sister kisses, or a chaste peck on the cheek. This lasted.

What came back was not sisterly, either.

THE MISSING TRACES

"...Those are all the notices which appeared before the disappearance of the bride."

"Before the what?" asked Holmes with a start.

"The vanishing of the lady."

Conan Doyle

"The Adventure of the Noble Bachelor"

CHAPTER 17

The Beginning

I walked down a deck or two, the taste of her lipstick still on my mouth, the look of her body still in my eyes, the curve of her back still on the tips of my fingers.

The smoking room was gloomy, despite all the subdued lighting they could turn on. It took a moment to make sure Tom was not here. Cotton-Hair Pennypacker, was though. He and his wife were playing bridge with two men and, when I saw who they were, I did a fast double-take. One man was Mesh-Gloves (and he still wore his gloves playing cards). The other was Dr. Cyclops. Even as I looked, Mrs. Pennypacker stood up and waved a protesting hand.

"No, no more," she said. "I must bathe and rest. Last night *was* strenuous you know, for an old lady."

Cotton-Hair Pennypacker caught sight of me. "How about it?" he called. "We're losing a player here. Won't you fill in for just one last rubber?"

I hadn't played bridge for five years. But this was one game I wanted to get into. Mrs. Pennypacker smiled at me, Mesh-Gloves and Cyclops each bowed to her stiffly and rather grumpily, making me wonder if she had won all the money, and Pennypacker performed introductions as she limped away. What had become of the Steak-Lovers?

"Mr.—ah, Deacon, right? It's your pal who is Dolan, isn't it? Yes. This is Mr. Bu, Mr. Deacon." Mr. Bu was Mesh-Gloves, and what nationality did that make him? He bowed, and did not shake hands. Maybe the gloves meant he had a painful skin disease.

"And Mr. Giorgione."

I felt like saying, "I've admired your paintings." Instead I shook hands and said I was glad to meet him, which was about half-true. He had an iron handshake that almost cracked my knuckles, but his hand was slimy-cold. Cyclops, or rather Mr. Giorgione now, said he was charmed. Maybe he was. One thing he surely wasn't, and that was Italian, despite his name.

"We have been playing for a cent a point," said Pennypacker. I was his partner now. He gathered in the cards and shuffled them with an easy, sure-fingered professionalism that made me remember Las Vegas. I began to wonder what I had let myself in for. Newt had said I would have an expense account. I suspected I'd need it.

As I said, I hadn't played bridge in some time, and I never was much competition for Charles Goren.

"For the last rubber," said Mr. Bu, and he looked down at his little mesh-gloved fingers clasped before him, "couldn't we go to five cents and make it a little more exciting?"

The accent was faintly oriental or Near Eastern.

Giorgione said nothing. His good eye was on Pennypacker's hands, shuffling the deck. The bad one was off in space.

"Choose?" said Pennypacker, fanning the deck out face down across the middle of the table. Every card overlapped the next by a mathematically perfect quarter of an inch.

I shrugged. "A nickel is fine."

"A nickel it is," Pennypacker said, and we picked cards. I drew the five of diamonds—a portent. I hoped Newt's bank had lots of money.

Bu won the deal with the queen of clubs, gathered in the cards, and presented them to me to cut. Then he passed them around with swift grace, the gloves obviously troubling him not at all.

I saw a waiter and waved. "I'd like a drink," I told the others. "Perhaps you'll have one with me."

"A Coke would be nice," said Pennypacker.

Giorgione merely nodded no, and frowned at his cards. I looked at Bu.

"No, thank you," he said. "I usually have sexual intercourse around six, and I never like to drink just before that."

I looked at him, then around at the others. No one seemed to have heard him or, if they had, paid him any particular attention. Then Pennypacker looked up at me quickly from his hand, grinned, and winked. *Live and learn.*

The rubber went fast—and badly for us. But halfway through I made a little progress.

* * * *

It came as it was my deal. I shuffled slowly and pretended to make conversation.

"That was quite a party last night. Or were you there?" I asked the question generally, and pushed the cards to Giorgione for cutting. "I know you were," I told Bu.

"Yes."

"But you didn't close the place up like we did. You were wise."

"We left quite early."

"That's the trouble with parties like that," said Pennypacker. "You want to stay on and on. Mama and I just looked in about ten o'clock, danced a few minutes, and then went below and read. We're that age, I guess."

I threw the cards around. "And you, *Signor* Giorgione? Dealer passes."

So far he had hardly opened his mouth. When he had his hand sorted, he studied it a moment. "One heart," he said and added absently, "I was not there."

"Another reader of books, no doubt," said Pennypacker. "Two diamonds, partner."

"And what were you reading?" I asked Giorgione, knowing the question would bother him.

"Two spades," said Bu.

"I wasn't reading," said Giorgione.

I had to look at my hand. I'd forgotten most of the rules for counting tricks. And I had no hand anyway. To hell with it—I wasn't here to win nickels. *Just don't trump any of your partner's aces, Deacon.*

"Three diamonds."

Giorgione said "Three hearts." Then he unexpectedly became voluble. "After dinner I went out on deck. It was beautiful—so dark and stormy. I ran into another passenger, an Indian, Mr. Vishnolar. We walked and talked. We have common interests. Some of the things he said excited me. And so, when I went below, I could not sleep. Even from the distance I could hear the orchestra playing for the party. Especially when they played the Dixieland music. I said my prayers twice, but for a long time I could not sleep. I think they should not have the parties so late."

His good eye glared indignantly, first at me and then at Bu.

"Five diamonds," said Pennypacker.

I wasn't paying much attention to him. How lucky can you get, I wondered. Two hours before, Tom and I had divided up some of the suspects for an alibi check, and now I had a pretty good idea where three of them were at the time of the maid's murder, or at least where they said they were, and Cotton-Hair Pennypacker to boot. If Tom had nailed down the other Penny-packer's alibi, as he surely must have, we were making progress.

Fortuitous progress.

Too fortuitous? Was it an accident that Giorgione and Vishnolar, the Indian, could alibi each other? Or that Bu sat near me for a time during the gala?

Everyone was looking at me. "I passed," said Bu impatiently.

What was the bid? I said, "Oh, yes," and pretended to study my cards. Pennypacker was smiling at me with bright-eyed encouragement. I had two diamonds in my hand, the higher being the five. I had the king of spades and the ten of hearts. Those were my high cards.

"Six diamonds," I said.

"Double," said Giorgione.

We went down four, doubled and vulnerable.

While Giorgione dealt, Pennypacker said philosophically, "Well, bridge is the great leveler, no matter who you are or what you do." He seemed not at all mad that I'd lost us fifty-five dollars each. "What else do you do, *Signor* Giorgione, aside from playing bridge very well?"

"I travel," said Giorgione.

Pennypacker looked at me and opened the bidding. "I pass."

I couldn't help laughing. "Giving up?"

He laughed back. "No. It was an honest appraisal of this hand."

"Never play cards with a magazine writer," I said. "We're totally ignorant of everything. Except what we're working on at the moment."

"Someone said you were with a magazine," he said.

I told him which one.

"Two spades," said Bu.

"You must travel a lot on stories," said Pennypacker.

"Yes. Pass. But right now it's for pleasure. Thank heaven."

"I know how you feel."

"Three hearts," said Giorgione.

"And you?" I said. "I gather you teach economics or business administration or something."

"Yes. Not now, though. I pass. On sabbatical. From Grinnell College. As you say, thank heaven."

"Amen."

"Five spades," said Bu, and Giorgione gave him the most frightful look I have ever seen at a bridge table.

Bu's hand played itself. He had everything, and made a grand slam in spades. It was so automatic that Pennypacker and I talked during the play.

"Maybe you can explain something to me," I said, just to keep the conversation going because I hoped to get to Bu. "Years ago I shared an apartment with another guy who was a broker. He claimed the best way to make money in the market was to deal in puts and calls and he even made it clear to me what those were. And he said the really great sure way to make money in the market was to straddle."

Pennypacker chuckled. "Puts and calls can save you a lot of grief," he said. "And make you a fair profit too, whichever way you go."

"But what's a straddle?"

"A straddle—" he glanced at his cards, then played one "—a straddle consists of buying two stocks of approximately the same value. It is based on certain technical evaluations of the stocks. They are never in the same category—two motors or two oils or anything like that."

"And then?"

"And then you play the rise or fall of one against the rise and fall of the other."

"I see. Maybe. Sounds intricate."

"It is."

"Slam in spades," said Bu.

Another hand ended the rubber. Pennypacker figured the winnings and losings. It turned out I had lost $105 of Newt Harlow's money.

Ho-hum.

With his winnings from the previous rubbers, Giorgione had won just under $210. "You play a beautiful game, sir," said Pennypacker, and I knew he meant it.

"I am half-asleep," said Giorgione. "Last night the party kept me awake. The night before I was awakened by some drunken lout arguing with his wife in a cabin nearby. Then they went out. I go back to sleep. They come back, and he is loudly complaining about the ship and its food and bumped into my door as he passed."

"You must be on the boat deck," I said.

"The boat deck," said Giorgione.

"I heard them roll in, too."

He and Pennypacker shook hands. Then he and I did. Then Pennypacker and I did. It was as formal as the preliminaries to a duel. Mesh-Gloves—Mr. Bu, I should call him now—did not. He bowed formally to all of us and left.

Anxious to get to his girlfriend, I thought. I went topside to the suite.

* * * *

A note on the table in Twit-Twit's handwriting said all three of them were at the movie. A snore from a bedroom told me Tom was making up for last night. I dropped down on my bed and thought that tonight Merrilee would be sleeping in it, and that made it difficult to even doze off.

But I did. Some time later, something was touching my hand. I awoke slowly, in darkness. My arm hung over the side of the bed, and something cold and wet was moving against my lingers. I thought of Giorgione's handshake.

It stopped and, at the same moment, it hit my chest with all four feet.

Stowaway, somewhere on the floor, had scented the food smells on my hand, started to lick it, and then leaped up and landed on my chest. Now she began walking up and down on me, like Captain Bligh striding the bridge, occasionally switching her tail in my face, and sometimes breathing sardine fumes at me.

"Lie down," I said. When I stroked her, she began to purr. She only purred when somebody stroked her. We both went to sleep.

The phone's jangle made both the cat and me jump; I found the phone in darkness.

A woman's voice said, "*M'sieu* Day-ah-cawn?" and I recognized the French pronunciation of my name.

"*Oui.*"

"You should come, please, to *le chambre de Mademoiselle* Moore. Something wrong."

"What's wrong?"

"Please come."

"Who is this?"

"The maid, *m'sieu.* After last night, the captain issue orders we are to pay special attention with *Mademoiselle* Moore. I come to check phone ringing. And she is not here. But I see something. There is something—"

"Something what?"

"There is a knock now at the door—it is the officer, I think. Please come, *m'sieu. Mademoiselle* told me you were the first to call if she had the trouble."

"She's not in the bathtub?"

"No, *m'sieu.*"

When I got to Merrilee's cabin, the first officer was also there. He looked worried.

"What's the problem?"

"The maid heard the phone ringing in here," he said. "Repeatedly. So she came in, after knocking several times."

"All right. But what's the trouble?"

"The trouble is *Mademoiselle* Moore is missing. The phone was the hairdresser. She had an appointment and did not arrive. She is not here, either. I ordered a check of the public rooms. She was paged. She is nowhere."

"She was going to the movie."

"She is definitely not in the movie."

"She is not in the bathroom?"

"No."

"How about the bedroom?"

"Marie knocked, then looked in."

I didn't knock, or look in. I opened the door and walked in. There was no one on the bed or in the room. It was very dark; the curtains had been drawn. But that is not what I first became aware of. There was a dressing table with a big mirror over it, partly behind the door. Just in front of the mirror, a candle was burning. Behind the candle on the mirror was Merrilee's face.

But it wasn't her face. It had been once. Now it was scarred and slashed, the sunken, dark-ringed eyes weirdly askew, the golden neck twisted and mutilated.

Then I recognized what I was looking at—a life-sized photograph of her face that had been cut out, retouched, and pasted on the mirror in horrid, sadistic caricature. In the candle's flickering, it was the first thing she would see when she walked into the room and closed the door. She would think she was seeing herself.

The first officer had not followed me into the bedroom. He said from the parlor, "I want to show you what alarmed the maid."

I went back out, closing the door behind me.

He was pointing to a place on the floor under a window. There was a little dark clot on the carpet. I leaned over it. It was blood. It was fresh.

I have never been so frightened.

What in God's name had they done?

Had they killed her? I couldn't believe it. But what was a girl's life against twenty-five or fifty million dollars, and a psychopath's enormous, revengeful bitterness?

"And if this is not enough," said the first officer, "the *m'sieu* Jones—her publicity man, yes?—he also 'as not been seen. His bed was not slept in. His steward reported it. And a passenger reported that a meat slicer—"

"Never mind the meat slicer. She is the important thing to find."

"But the meat slicer 'as been found, *m'sieu*. Outside a passenger's door. A *M'sieu* Pennypackair. He reported it to us. With a piece of rope—all sticky with green paint—someone left in his room. *M'sieu* Pennypackair was most indignant."

"You'd better search the ship. Right away." I think my voice sounded odd. "Completely. If she is not on it—I don't know where we go from there."

I thought of something else. They obviously did not know what was in the bedroom; the maid had only glanced in and not looked behind the door. It was better if they did not know. And Merrilee surely must not see it.

"I'll start the search right now," I said. "I didn't look in her closet."

I went back into the bedroom, snuffed out the candle, and stripped the photo from the mirror, trying not to handle it any more than necessary for the sake of fingerprints. The rubber cement that held it was still fresh-smelling. I folded it and put it in my pocket. Then I looked in the closet, saw only clothes, came out, and said, "Nothing doing."

The maid looked terrified.

The first officer and I stepped out into the corridor.

"You are right," he said. "We must search every part of the ship. At once."

"At once."

The maid came out into the corridor. "I called the *coiffeur* again," she said. "She has *non* arrive."

"Let's get going," I told the officer. "What can I do to help?"

"Nothing, *m'sieu.* The search is for the crew. I will call you within thirty minutes in your cabin."

He looked frightened. I suppose I did, too. Things were coming to a climax, and I had a feeling I wouldn't like the climax.

In the suite, I heard Tom's snores and saw our whiskey bottle. But I didn't want a drink. I didn't want anything except the knowledge that Merrilee was somewhere aboard and somehow okay.

I began pacing the floor.

CHAPTER 18

The Corpse

As I paced, I swayed a little, and at first I figured that my footing was uncertain because I was nervous. And I was. In a crisis inaction is the crudest torture.

But after a few minutes I realized the reason I was swaying was not nervousness. It was the ship.

Outside, the wind was beginning to growl and howl alternately. The forward rises and plunges were perhaps a little heavier than before, but they were not so noticeable because she was rolling so deeply from side to side. Things moved and slid by themselves on the bureaus and desk, and water slopped out of the carafe by my bed. In the closets, clothes on hangers made brushing sounds and clinking noises.

This was heavy weather.

I looked out a window. All you saw was flying gray water and watery-gray light, and you could not tell where the sea stopped and the sky began.

The door to the suite swung suddenly open, and I thought the storm had done that, too, but Twit-Twit lurched in and slammed it shut.

"God help the poor sailor on a night like this," she said.

"Have you seen Merrilee?"

"Why are you so anxious about Merrilee? I almost broke my ankle on the—"

"Haven't you heard the news?"

"What news? I damn near break my neck going up the stairs to get up here—they've got ropes all over the place, but they don't help much—and the first thing I hear—"

"God damn it, Twit, tell me. Where did you last see her?" She surveyed me.

"Why is it so important at this moment?"

"Because the whole ship is being hunted for her. She may have gone overboard."

Twit-Twit looked at me searchingly. "You mean it. Something's really wrong."

"Something is God-damned wrong. She may have been killed. There's a bloodstain in her cabin. She may—please tell me when you last saw her."

She said, "I'm sorry. I last saw her at the movie."

"Which just let out?"

"Yes."

"But they've been hunting her for half an hour. All over the ship."

"That must be what the paging meant."

"What paging?"

"She and I and Bets met at the movie. Marlon Brando in—"

"Screw Marlon Brando."

"We'd hardly sat down when they paged her. You know. Over the PA system."

"And?"

"She sort of scrounged up next to me and said, 'Now what do they want?' I said that maybe it was a cable or something. She said she didn't want any cables. She seemed scared."

"It figures."

"I guess so. Anyway, she said, 'I just want to stay here and see the picture.' But after a little while they paged her again, and in a few moments she whispered she had a date at the hairdresser, and got up and left. Quite suddenly. Bets and I stayed until the end."

Was she back in her cabin?

I picked up the phone and dialed Cabin B-78. It didn't answer.

I found the *coiffeur* in the ship's telephone list and dialed that.

"Did Miss Moore get in yet?"

"Who is calling, *m'sieu*?"

"This is the bridge," I lied. "*M'sieu* Deacon. I am calling for the captain, who is alarmed."

"*Oui, m'sieu. J'ai compris. Mademoiselle Moore n'a pas apparue.*"

"*Merci.*" I rang off. "No dice. Twit—I'm scared."

She patted my arm. Through the wall from the cabin next to us, there came the bull-like bellowing of Mr. Steak-Lover, roaring angrily at his wife. Twit-Twit said, "Don't panic yet. They'll turn her up. Just wait until all the returns are in." The telephone rang in my hand; I'd never released my grip on it.

"Yes?"

"Mr. Deacon?" It was a woman's voice. But not the right one.

"Yes?"

"I have a transatlantic call for you. One moment."

It was several moments. Then Newt's voice broke in. "Hello? Hello? Deac?"

"Yes. What's up?"

"Well, I'll tell you. I am definitely going to buzz over to London and meet all of you when you land at Southampton."

"That may be a good idea." I wondered how to break the news. "In fact, it *is* a good idea. I just hope we're all there to meet you."

"How do you mean?"

"Merrilee is missing," I said. I couldn't think of any kinder way to say it.

"What do you mean, missing?" Fear raised his voice half an octave.

"She went to the movie this afternoon. Left early to go to the hairdresser. She never got there. The entire ship is being searched right now. So far, no dice."

I have never heard so long a silence.

"You think they got her some way?"

"Somebody's hid her away, at least."

"But on a ship—there are only so many places."

"On a ship there is always the ocean."

There was another long silence.

"Blame me for it. But God, Newt, she was even at a movie with friends of mine. Before that, we had all lunched together. And she'd been thoroughly put on guard."

"Stop it. I blame myself. We should have shipped her to Europe in a lead container, like uranium, surrounded by twenty-five uniformed cops. But where—? Do you have any ideas about who 'they' are—the ones on the ship?"

"Oh, yes. But revenge or punishment won't—if they've—if they've hurt her."

"You sound in a bad way."

"I may kill somebody before I get off this boat."

Twit-Twit's eyes widened.

Newt said, "Now for Almighty God's sake, Deac, don't get Irish and crazy."

"I won't," I said, "because I have no real proof right now. This is a hell of a clever operator, and he has good help. Tell you one thing you can do."

"Right."

"Do you have this morning's paper handy?"

"Sure."

"Look in the sports pages and tell me who won yesterday's ball game between the Mets and the Dodgers."

"For the love of heaven! Is this a time to worry about baseball?"

"Do what I said. I just want the final score."

"Just a minute." A pause. Then, "The Dodgers won, four to one."

"Are you sure you've got the right paper? And the right date and game? It was yesterday's game. The opener."

"Sure. Right here in the *New York Times.*"

"Four to one."

"That was the score."

"That may help quite a lot."

"What *are* you talking about?"

"Never mind now."

"Call me as soon as you get a report—no matter how bad it is. You have my home number."

We hung up.

Twit-Twit and I exchanged looks. I suppose how I felt showed in my face. She came forward and put her arms around me. She didn't kiss me or anything. It's the sort of thing that made me fall in love with Twit-Twit.

"Relax a minute," she said. "Then we'll figure what to do next. And what I can do to help."

"You'll stay here and answer the phone."

"While you—?"

"While I communicate with these bastards."

"You mean, the people who—?"

"Yes. I can send them a message. It may help. It can't do any harm."

"Where's Tom?"

"In his room, asleep. Call on him if you need anything. Where's Betsy?"

"She was going to do a little shopping in the *boutique*, then come right up here."

"I'll be back in a few minutes."

"Do I have time to change and get into something loose?"

"Of course. All you have to do is listen for the phone. Or a knock at the door."

"I'll even leave the john door open."

"You don't have to be indelicate."

But I kissed her and left.

* * * *

Walking around the passageway to Merrilee's suite, I thought about what I would say. I could not risk overstating my case, because my case wasn't that strong, even though it was shaping up. But if it was going to help her—if, indeed, it *could* help her—I had to make it convincing.

No one was on guard in front of her cabin. I used the key and stepped inside and, as I did, a silly, wistful hope flashed across my mind—that somehow she would be there, dressed or undressed, or maybe making splashing noises in the tub. But there was no sound at all. I closed the door carefully and went directly to the day bed.

All I had to do was switch the bug on, perhaps give it a minute to warm up, and then talk into it. They'd get the message, all right. Immediately, or by tape, or however they worked it.

I pulled the covers back and reached. And that was all.

The bug was not there.

I took the elevator back up to the suite. As I swung into our corridor, I saw the first officer standing at our door. He pushed the button.

Twit-Twit opened the door promptly.

"*M'sieu* Deacon. Is he in?" the first officer asked.

"I guess he is now," said Twit-Twit.

I said, "Hi." We went inside.

Tom was sitting in a chair in shirt-sleeves and slacks, looking deliberately sleepy, from which I knew he was very much awake.

"What's the news?" I said.

"It is not good, *m'sieu*," the first officer said. He held his cap in his hands apologetically. "It is—it is not at all good." He was excessively polite, as though he felt he were to blame.

"Then what is it?"

The deep-pile carpeting we stood on rose and sank beneath us as the ship plowed and rolled. The parlor's subdued lighting was oppressive, like that in a funeral home. Suddenly I wanted a strong, heady drink, or a cigarette (I don't smoke), or a change of scene—like an English moor. Illogical, but real.

"It is—we've found something, *m'sieu*."

"Well, Christ! *What*?"

"The search is not complete. The men—we even brought out the night crews to—how you say?—expedite *l'affaire*. The men 'ave gone over the ship, except for the lowest part, where is the propeller shaft. They are going through that now."

"But you said—"

From the wall behind me came a loud bumping sound in the next cabin. It was the storm, moving furniture around, or Steak-Lover bouncing his wife off the wall.

"*M'sieu*, you are a friend of *Mademoiselle* Moore. You are associated with her."

"Yes."

"Perhaps you feel a—responsible for her?"

"In a way. What are you driving at?"

He seemed to summon his courage. Tom was watching him like a judge watches the key witness at a murder trial. Twit-Twit had gone into her room, but I could see by a shadow on the wall that she was eavesdropping just inside her door.

"We 'ave found the body, *m'sieu.*"

I died, and he saw it.

"Oh, not hers. But one of her associates. The *M'sieu* Jones? In a lifeboat. Like the maid."

CHAPTER 19

The Middle

I said, "Oh?"

"You knew him, *m'sieu*?"

"Slightly. A bar acquaintance."

"That is two, of course. Of the friends of the *mademoiselle*. It is—it is most ominous."

"Yes."

The first officer looked around, carefully not seeing Tom. "Can we speak alone, *m'sieu*?"

Tom said, "Pardon me. See you later," and went into his room.

The first officer bowed acceptance in his direction and spoke lower. He did not see Twit-Twit's shadow.

"*M'sieu. M'sieu* Jones was murdered. Slugged and 'anged. But obviously he was not 'anged in a lifeboat. No. So in my opinion to solve this matter is not only to find the person who kills people, but to ascertain why put them in lifeboats. Someone who thinks he may get off the boat before they are even found, perhaps."

"Yes."

Twit-Twit's shadow was still there. The first officer was still looking elaborately away from me, yet our glances met. Because he was watching me, and had been all the time, in the mirror over the Louis XIV commode. He looked away.

"His steward 'as told me you wanted to get into his cabin early yesterday."

That one I was ready for.

"Yes. We had had a nightcap at the bar, and I mentioned I like to take a turn around the deck early in the morning. He said he would like that too, and asked me to knock at his door. So I did. When he did not answer, I became a little worried—he had had a lot to drink. I asked the steward to look in, just to see if he was all right. That was all."

"I see."

"Are you checking alibis, or anything like that?"

"*M'sieu!* At least, not here."

"Then where, if you don't mind my asking?"

"Nowhere, yet."

"Has the news gone out to—the rest of the world?"

"Only to our headquarters in Le Havre. A secret."

And how long would it stay a secret there?

"Just one thing, since we were speaking of alibis." I was, anyway. "I gather the maid must have been killed last night during the gala. Have you determined a time of death, or figured out who was at the gala and who wasn't all evening?"

"It would be impossible, *m'sieu.* People go in and out. Except people like you and me. We both know we were there all evening."

"Oh, of course."

So I had an alibi. Or so he thought. Or so he wanted me to think he thought. And he had one too. Or so he wanted me to think.

"*M'sieu.* I must ask a favor."

"Of course."

"There is one part of the ship we 'ave not searched."

"Her stateroom?"

"No, *m'sieu.* Yours. Your suite. May I?"

I saw Twit-Twit's shadow vanish.

"Please do, by all means."

"It is just that—a formality."

"Of course. I had just better warn Miss Twickenham." Twit-Twit was coolly creaming her face at the make-up table when I looked in. "Visitor," I said.

He excused himself abjectly, then looked carefully in the closet, around the bathroom, and under the bed. He even glanced into the life-preserver rack. Then he did Tom's room. If the entire search of the ship was like that, it would be impossible for them to overlook a five-pound sack of flour.

Back in the parlor, I said, "Now I'd like you to give me a hand with something."

"*M'sieu?*"

"It involves the ship personnel, and may have something to do with Miss Moore's disappearance."

His glance narrowed. "*Oui?*"

"I want to talk to the man who runs the ship's newspaper. I'll do the talking. But I want you there to scare him. To make him think his job is in danger."

"Beaubien?" He sounded thunderstruck.

"If that's the printer. Could we do it now?"

"He would be 'aving *dîner.* Below. Far below."

"Then let's go see him."

"*Oui, m'sieu.*"

I went to Tom's bedroom door. "I'm going out for a few minutes. Will you or Twit-Twit be here?"

"Sure."

"It's important that someone be in here to take messages."

"I dig."

"Back in fifteen minutes."

We went down, down, down in the elevator and then by stairs. Finally he led me through a narrow, rather grimy, corridor and opened an unmarked door. It was a small wardroom, apparently below the waterline. Half a dozen crewmen were scattered at several clothless tables, eating. A bottle of red wine stood on each table.

One of those eating was the printer. He saw us bearing down on him and looked alarmed. He got to his feet, rubbing his mouth with a paper napkin.

"This gentleman wants to talk to you," the first officer said shortly.

"*M'sieu?*"

"I want the truth about the baseball score."

"*M'sieu?* Baseball score?"

"You know what I mean."

"I do not understand the *anglais* very good, *m'sieu.*"

"Yes, you do." I spoke slowly. "This is a police matter. You understand that, don't you? I want the truth about that baseball score I asked you about earlier today. The truth. Start talking."

The first officer said nothing. He stood with folded arms, frowning at the printer. He didn't know what I was talking about, but he was playing his part.

The printer touched his lips again with the napkin.

"I-I—"

"The truth, immediately," I said. "Or the police in Le Havre."

"Immediately, Beaubien!" The first officer echoed.

"I—*oui.* Yes. I change the score. The—how was it?—the Dodgairs against the Mets. It is true."

"Why did you do it?"

"I receive a letter."

"From whom?"

"I do not know, m'sieu. It was dropped in the mailbox on the door of my printing shop. I found it yesterday evening."

"And?"

"There was a five-hundred-franc note. And the letter said the writer 'ad made a joking bet on the baseball score with a friend. He want me to make it a certain numbers in the paper. And if I did, there would be another five-hundred-franc note."

"And so you did."

He shrugged. He did not look at the first officer. "What difference makes a baseball score, *m'sieu*?" He did not look at me either. "I am sorry if it was wrong."

One thousand francs. About two hundred dollars. The first officer said, "Did you save the letter you received?"

"No, *m'sieu le commandant.*"

"Where is it now?" I asked.

He gestured toward the empty wastebasket and shrugged.

"And did you get the other five hundred francs?"

"Not yet, *m'sieu.*"

That was interesting. Were they simply cheating him? Or playing things doubly safe?

"When you get it," I said, "if you do, preserve everything. The envelope it comes in. The franc note. Everything. You can have the money. But we want every bit of evidence we can get."

He shook his head emphatically yes.

"Bring it," said the first officer, "to me. If you get it and do not bring it at once—" He smiled sardonically and made that wonderful little Gallic gesture, a flick of the wrist at waist level, which says so much. Among other things, *you know how things happen.*

As we went out, I looked back at the printer. He had sat down and, hands on knees, was staring into his plate un-hungrily.

CHAPTER 20

The Ending

But what he had said made me think of the metal mailbox, with a hinged top, that I had noticed on the printshop door. And also of something I had learned years ago as a police reporter on a newspaper. I said to the first officer, "Can we go to the ship's doctor, quickly? I want a lot of aspirin, and some light oil. But let's hurry—we may be too late even now."

"Are you ill, *m'sieu?*"

"No—I've got a crazy idea. That five-hundred-franc bribe will be paid, I think. And the person who drops it in the printer's mailbox is the person we are hunting. He will leave his mark on the metal box."

"Fingerprints?"

"Fingerprints are uncertain, no matter what you may have heard. What I have in mind is far more certain."

We reached the doctor's office fast because the first officer commandeered the elevator, and there I ground three dozen aspirin tablets to powder, using some tongue depressors and a metal bowl. We borrowed a little bottle of mineral oil, took the elevator down, and hurried to the printshop.

I coated its hinged metal cover lightly with the oil, then blew aspirin dust all over it. I wiped away the excess that had blown onto the rest of the box so that the top now looked as if it had been painted a sort of grayish-white. I said a silent prayer that it would work.

As we walked down a main-deck corridor toward the purser's office, the first officer said, "M'sieu, I do not understand any of this, but especially I do not understand why someone would wish—would want to 'ave the baseball score fabricated."

"It was part of a plot to frighten her. To make her return to America."

"I do not understand."

"It's an involved story. I don't know much about it myself, movie-business rivalry. I'd rather explain what I know of it a little later."

We were going up the stairs to the main deck when he spoke again, impulsively. "*M'sieu, M'sieu* Jones's face, when he was found, had been painted green."

"Painted?"

"Yes. Could that be connected with the plot to frighten *Mademoiselle* Moore?"

"I don't know. Maybe."

The assistant purser, in charge of the ship's office, was young and efficient-looking.

"Is the report final?" the first officer asked.

"*Je viens de rapporter à la passerelle.*"

"You may speak in English."

The assistant purser looked at me curiously. "I have just informed the bridge. The search is complete. She is not aboard."

"Not a sign?" I asked. "Of anything?"

"Not a sign, *m'sieu*. She never got to *le coiffeur*. A woman who left the cinema just behind her said the *Mademoiselle* Moore started for the main staircase and began walking up."

"Toward the boat deck."

"Or the *coiffeur*. No one has reported seeing her after that. There is no trace of—anything."

"The search must be done again. At once."

I felt the same way. Not because a second search was likely to result differently. But because it was something to have going, a last tatter of hope to cling to. Anything was better than this feeling of steady sinking into catastrophe.

"The captain has already ordered it," the purser said. "The men are being held."

"I will direct," the first officer said.

"God damn it."

I didn't say it to anyone in particular except, perhaps, to myself. "She's got to be—she's *got* to be someplace!"

They looked at each other.

"Someplace aboard, I mean."

"These things somehow—they can happen, *m'sieu*," the young purser said.

Solemnity lengthened the first officer's lean dark face. "Do not abandon hope. We will do everything that can be done. I will call you on the instant of news."

* * * *

In our suite, Tom had done what he could, too. He had ordered two double Martinis; they stood on a little table between the lounge chairs.

"I can tell by your face," he said.

I sat down. "The search is over. She's not on the ship. That's all. She's not on the ship."

"Drink that."

I took a gulp. "They're doing the whole search once more. But it's routine. They've gone over every inch once. Carefully."

I leaned back and closed my eyes. After a long while I opened them again and drank more Martini. It could have been water.

"I think the most that can happen now," I said, "is that the second search may turn up some indication of how she—of what happened to her. Where are the women?"

"Twit-Twit was going to shower. Bets came in just before you did. She's lying down. I think she'd been crying."

"Crying?"

"She'd heard a report on the search. She liked Merrilee."

I closed my eyes again. When I opened them, Tom was finishing his Martini. I finished mine.

Tom said, "You know, to begin with, you did a lot more than you were supposed to do. Right from the start."

"I didn't do enough."

He said, "Just for the hell of it, let's go over the alibis we rounded up, such as they may be."

"That's not the real problem. The real problem is, she's gone. Revenge is easy. Like punishment. Restoring a human life is impossible."

"We'll have two more drinks." He rang for the steward. "Let's compare notes anyway. You probably got more than I did."

I recognized what he was trying to do for me. It was probably useless, but anything was better than imagining the way of her death. Aboard ship, in a sudden confrontation? Or in the cold, heaving sea, in a welter of despair?

"You start."

I tried. "I haven't got so much. I did have one piece of luck," and I told him about the bridge game.

"So if what this Cyclops—his real name is Giorgione—says is true, his meeting on deck with the Indian alibis not only himself but the Indian. His alibi for the first night isn't much, although it's convincing."

"Then there's the kid in the mesh gloves, Mr. Bu. He sat next to us during part of the gala. He said he and his lovely girlfriend left early, but early was a long time after midnight, as I remember. What he was doing the first night I don't know."

"The first officer?"

"He indicates he has an alibi. He doesn't, any more than I do. How was your luck with Widow's-Peak Pennypacker?"

"Good and bad. Good because, oddly enough, he said he will make a guest appearance on the show next fall and really talk facts. He's a vain bastard, and I think you're right about the fag part. He says he must appear in a mask, because he cannot afford personal recognition."

"That figures."

"Yes. Anyway, he said last night at the gala he was there and sat alone, near the college girls. He danced with some of them, including the chaperone. It seemed to amuse him."

"I saw him. But in that crowd anyone could have been there and gone and come back without being noticed by someone else."

"The first night he said he had quite a few cocktails and then drank a bottle of sparkling Burgundy all by himself at dinner. He said he went to bed stoned, around ten-thirty."

"That seems to be that. Everybody has an alibi. Or else doesn't."

"Yes. How about that other Pennypacker—Old Grandad? He's so damned wholesome, I sometimes—the coincidence of names is odd."

"Odd, but it's how things happen in real life. Anyway, at bridge this afternoon he said he and his wife looked in on the gala a few minutes, danced, and then left to go below and read. The first night I know he was playing bridge in the smoking lounge when we came up here, because I saw him."

"I have a feeling we don't suspect the right people." He pushed the steward's button in sudden irritation.

From out in the corridor came the voice of Steak-Lover, bellowing at his wife. "When he comes back with decent sheets, you tell that steward we want some drinking water. *Clean!* Or no tip Friday." The door slammed and he clumped down the hall.

Tom said, "I take it the steward is otherwise engaged. I'll go up to the bar myself." And he went.

I sat there while it got darker. That's not merely a literal statement. The expensive cloisonné lamps spread subdued light, but a hundred million candle-power could not have brightened that room.

Twit-Twit came to her door. I didn't feel like talking.

"Don't look like that. And don't feel like it, darling."

"Okay."

She walked to me fast on flapping mules and kissed me. But like the Martini, it didn't do what it usually did.

"I'm not going to shower. I'm going to take you to the bar and buy you a drink."

"Everyone's buying me a drink. Tom's gone for some now. You shower."

"Sure?"

"A drink won't help. Knowing the way you feel does, though."

She kissed me again and left, slender in the negligee.

* * * *

I knew what I would ultimately do. I didn't know or care how I would do it. Twit-Twit's shower hissed on loud, then softer. The ship surmounted a tremendous wave, then seemed to crash down into the trough, the woodwork groaned in torture, and water in hidden pipes gasped obscenely.

This was an end of things. I wanted Tom to come back with the Martinis. Or with none. I didn't care if I never had a drink, or if I had a million. I just wanted something to change; if the ship had sunk at that moment, it would have been fine.

There was a light knock at the door.

I said, "Come in."

The first officer opened it. He took one pace into the parlor. An expressionless crewman stood outside.

"*M'sieu.*"

We looked at each other. I think at that moment we hated each other.

"*M'sieu.* The second search is complete. She is not aboard. It is certain."

I didn't try to talk; there was all the time left in eternity in which to say things. I finally said, "Thanks for letting me know. Personally."

Only revenge was left.

"Do you know, *m'sieu*...her relatives must be notified. Do you know where they are?"

"She had none. Not even an ex-husband. And her mother is dead. Nothing can be done now."

"*Mais oui.*" He touched his cap and the door closed behind him, leaving a vacuum.

* * * *

After a time I got up and turned off all the lights. Maybe I was trying to hide from myself.

It was sightlessly dark in the room. I wanted company. No, I didn't want company. The cat purred from somewhere. I wanted—I didn't know what I wanted.

"Here, cat. Here, Stowaway. Where are you?"

The purring stopped. Then it started again. Storm noise drowned it out; then I heard it, distantly. Then it was drowned out.

In one of the bedrooms? Both doors were closed. I listened at each. No.

The purring was louder in the parlor. I fumbled for my flashlight on the night stand and walked around slowly, making a game of it, snapping the light on periodically to look on the bed and under it, around the chairs, even in the life-belt rack. The purring was loudest at the closet door.

"Come out. Come out, Stowaway."

The purring stopped abruptly, and I fumbled for the doorknob.

As I did, rockets flashed, my heart stopped, a million cannon exploded. *The cat never purred except when it was petted.*

The first officer had searched the entire suite—but not this parlor closet.

I wrenched the door open and shafted the flashlight down. There was the cat, blinking in the sudden light, tail curled under her, lying on the stomach of someone sprawled on the closet floor.

The someone smiled a beautiful, sleepy smile. Her spun-gold hair was tousled childishly.

"I've had such a nice nap among your shoes," said Merrilee. "What time is it?"

She stroked the cat again, and the cat began to purr again.

I helped her up. I held her. I kissed her—almost tearfully.

"How the hell long have you been here?"

"I don't know. I went to sleep."

"Since you left the movie?"

"No. The movie is where I got scared—when they started paging me. After a while I couldn't sit still. If they were going to hurt me, they might hurt your friends, too. I just wanted to hide somewhere. I had the key you gave me. So I started up the stairs for here.

"But the public-address system kept paging me and I—I panicked. I didn't even get this far; I ducked into the ladies' room down the hall and just—just sat in one of the booths. For over half an hour. I took a tranquilizer."

"Don't you know they searched the whole damned ship for you, twice—from keel to crow's-nest? *Twice*!"

"Twice? Gee! That shows they *do* care, doesn't it?"

She meant it. I was so relieved I wanted to slap her—with love.

"That must be why this woman came into the john and called out my name."

"It probably was a maid."

"I thought she might be one of those hunting me. That's what gave me the nerve to leave. I got your key all ready and peeked out. No one was in sight. I ran like a bunny down the corridor and let myself in. No one was around except your friend Tom, on the bed."

This, of course, would be after I had left with the first officer and before the women came in.

"I tiptoed around and found I could be comfortable in the closet. Honest—your loafers are as soft as any pillow. The cat came in with me. She's cute. I took another tranquilizer and went to sleep.

"After a while I heard you and your friend talking, but far away. When I woke up just now I felt safe and comfortable. I patted the cat. She likes me."

Even while she talked, I was thinking far beyond this immediate situation. Thank heaven I had given her the key. Quite aside from possibly protecting her, it had begun a series of events that could miraculously change things. We'd keep her here. No one but ourselves—*no one*—would know. What *that* would do to the opposition!

They knew she was gone. But they knew they didn't have her, and had not killed her. Had their terror tactics worked so that she had killed herself? They might think so, and act accordingly.

The hall door kicked open. Tom stood in the doorway, holding two large Martinis. He looked at her for ten long seconds, then came forward.

He handed her one drink. She smiled her thanks.

His eyes never leaving her, Tom drank the other one nonstop.

THE ULTIMATE TRACES

"There! there!" said Holmes, soothingly, patting him upon the shoulder. "It was too bad to spring it on you like this; but Watson here will tell you that I never can resist a touch of the dramatic."

—Arthur Conan Doyle
"The Naval Treaty"

CHAPTER 21

Night Watch

Betsy and Twit-Twit came out of their rooms in response to Tom's knocks, and I won't try to describe their expressions. I locked the outside door and we sat babbling light-headedly for a couple of minutes.

Above all, there was the wonderful sense of relief.

And Merrilee's touching gratitude, like that of a little girl attending the first birthday party ever held for her, that we had been grieved and frightened.

The instant I had seen her I began to get, for the first time, the scent of victory. I did not dare say what was in my mind, because it might cause something to show in their faces before the night was out.

So, during those few minutes of happy conversation, I mentioned only that I thought it might be better if we had dinner by ourselves in the suite and kept Merrilee's presence a secret from everyone, especially the waiter and steward.

"One other thing," I said. "If you'll just take my word for it, it's kind of important that we keep a close watch on the radio shack."

"Why?" said Tom.

"Because the opposition may send a message very quickly. Perhaps it has already. Maybe not. I need to know who sends it, or by what intermediary."

"So?"

"I'm going topside and camp near the radio office. All of you stay here, order another drink, and then dinner. But order only for four. And when the waiter comes, Merrilee, you be well out of sight so he doesn't see you. Like in the closet."

She made an impish smile.

"You can take the cat if you like. But all order generously, because we must make four dinners do for five people. After you four have eaten, Tom will come up and spell me while I grab a bite. Dine well. This is going to be a heavy night."

But the dinner-by-turns proved unnecessary.

I went up to the dark sun deck, pulled a deck chair into a far corner, and slouched in it with my coat pulled up around my ears. It was cold, with spatters of rain and salt spray, and the ship was pitching with regular irregularity. But I didn't care. The end was approaching and, as I lay watching for whoever might approach the radio shack and wondering whether he (or she?) already had, I thought of bits of stagecraft that might help us. One I liked particularly.

Then a tall muffled figure came up the little port-side stair and moved toward the bridge. He walked head down into the gale. It was the first officer.

I got up and yelled "Hey!" not too loudly, and he wheeled.

"Do me a favor. In the Merrilee Moore investigation."

"*M'sieu!*"

I'd startled him.

"I want to know who sent or received cables, or made telephone calls from the ship, since around four o'clock. I know that's a lot to ask. But I'm not prying into other people's personal affairs. I'm gradually locating the person responsible for Miss Moore's disappearance and also for two murders."

We surveyed each other a long moment. Perhaps the light wasn't very good. Then he said, "Come," and walked into the radio shack.

He talked in French with the radio officer and turned to me with a sheaf of papers.

"There 'as been only one telephone this afternoon, *m'sieu,*" he said. "It was to Beirut, this telephone, and it was made by a passenger, a Lebanese, who deals in oil and travels with us often. I think probably not important."

"I think probably not. The cables?"

"It is understood you 'ave never seen them?"

"It is understood." He handed me five paper flimsies.

Two were to the same Wall Street broker from the same name and ordered sales of two batches of the same stock. The third read:

YOUR WINE MADE MY DINNER STOP MUCH LOVE STOP ABBY

That one I handed back to him. Somebody aboard had been cabled some wine. "You can check later if someone named Abby received the wine."

"I can check now." He talked to the radio man and got a considerable reply in French.

"It seems this is the young lady in charge of the other young-lady students—their chaperone. The telegrapher received the wine order yesterday by the wireless and *Mademoiselle* Elwyn herself sent the reply from here this afternoon."

"Okay."

I looked at the next one. It was brief and pointed, and it was addressed to what sounded like a legal firm, at a midtown New York address.

HEREWITH RESIGNATION STOP WHOEVER YOU ARE STOP PENNYPACKER

I read the last one. It was addressed to a small Scottish village outside Edinburgh, and read tersely:

ARRIVE MONDAY WEEK STOP MACKENZIE

It sounded authentic.

"Will you arrange for me to see whatever other messages are sent to-night?"

He looked unhappy, shrugged the French shrug, spoke to the radio man, who looked at me and said, "*Oui, m'sieu*," and we left.

I thanked him; he looked uncomfortable and headed for the bridge, and I went to the chair I had occupied to put it back in the rack. As I lifted it, someone else came up the starboard ladder and clattered lamely on high heels across the deck toward the radio office.

It was Mrs. Cotton-Hair Pennypacker.

When she'd gone inside, I put the chair down softly and waited in my corner, glad that my topcoat was dark blue. She came out and ducked hur-riedly down the ladder. I went back into the radio office and held out my hand. The radio man handed me the message she had just turned in.

It was addressed to one John Schneider at the New York office of Roger Kane Productions and said simply:

LOVELY TRIP STOP ALL IS WELL EDITH

"Thank you."

He saluted gravely, and I said that I might be back a little later, and he smiled with good humor. I went back to our suite, feeling pretty good.

They had ordered more than enough for five people and were into the *profiteroles* when I came in. I squeezed a chair into a corner of the table set for four, sipped a glass of Montrachet, and told Tom to forget about the watch on the radio shack. Now we had more interesting things to do. There was lobster mayonnaise, with a rack of lamb and Chambertin to follow; I ate hungrily.

It was getting on to nine-thirty when we finished and upended the wine bottles in the ice buckets.

"I have a little errand," I said. "Won't take a minute. Tom, want to come along?"

I explained what I had in mind on the way to the smoking room. I also asked him a question.

"Look, you know everything about the market."

"I do?"

"Sure. So what's a 'straddle'?"

"Well, it's relatively rare and usually occurs when someone playing the market has a strong hunch or information that a certain stock is definitely going up or definitely down. The straddle gives the speculator a chance to profit either way."

"That's nice."

"To put it simply for mental giants like yourself, the speculator buys an option to buy a certain number of shares of a given stock at a future date at a certain price. And at the same time, he buys *another* option—to sell the same amount of the same stock at the same future date at the same price."

"It sounds like a complicated road to nowhere."

"Not if the stock is volatile, as we say in the street. Suppose the straddle is for six months. In that time, the stock may go down, and the straddler can buy it more cheaply than the specified option price. So he makes money if it goes back up. And if it goes up far enough, then he will also make money when he buys at the specified price. And the reverse is also true."

"I think I get it, but don't try to explain the reverse, or I'll fall off."

"It's a rather unusual stock-market maneuver," said Tom, "but familiar enough to money men."

In the smoking room, we bought two decks of ship's cards from the steward, and Tom bought us into the ship's pool again because he said he felt this was a lucky night. I wondered if he was right.

Then he went back to the suite to figure out exactly what needed to be done to the cards, and I went hunting.

It wasn't easy. Not because the quarry was hard to track down, but because the storm was approaching a climax. Even using the lines strung on the stairways, you had to walk—and sometimes were compelled to run-in a quick-footed crouch, and the ship's personnel all wore the fixed mechanical smiles of men under strain. I tried the dining salon first and scored immediately.

The room was half-empty. Not many passengers felt hungry tonight. Cotton-Hair Pennypacker was there, with Steak-Lover and his wife, both of whom were eating broiled lobster for once, over great white bibs tucked under their respective chins. Mr. Bu and his breath-taking friend were at a nearby table and, farther away, the other Pennypacker.

I went to Cotton-Hair's table. "We had dinner at home tonight," I said. "Our lady friends are not feeling too well. None of us are. So Tom and I were thinking of a little poker to cheer us up. Do you ever give up bridge for poker?"

"Well now, there's just nothing I like better than a little session of poker," said Cotton-Hair. "And you are certainly entitled to a chance to recoup. Dear, you'll excuse me, I'm sure."

"I'd rather read my mystery novel anyway," she said.

"Care to join us?" I asked Steak-Lover.

"Maybe. But not until I've finished dessert." The words came slowly out of a mouth filled with lobster.

I caught Bu's eye and made card-dealing motions with my hands and asked a question with my eyebrows. He nodded yes. His girlfriend kept her eyes demurely on her plate.

Widow's-Peak Pennypacker was watching me out of the corner of his left ear. "Poker?" I called. It was a goofy and unexpected chance.

He spread cheese on a piece of bread, then looked up again. "Maybe. What time?"

"Let's say ten-thirty. In the smoking room."

He waved assent. "Ten-thirty it is."

"Ten-thirty," Cotton-Hair said.

I left. As I did, I spotted the college girls' chaperone, still enjoying her wine. In fact, she looked extremely happy. I felt better than she did, though. I'd rounded up quite a few.

And we'd round up a few more.

CHAPTER 22

The Monster

The maid knocked at ten to make down the beds, and we hurriedly bundled Merrilee into the closet. While the maid worked, Tom stood in front of the closet door to prevent slipups. There weren't any and, when she had left, I said, "You all have assignments. Merrilee, yours is to stay out of sight in this suite until a certain time, as I'll explain. Tom knows what he has to do. Betsy and Twit-Twit are in charge of communications."

"Which means?" Betsy said.

"Which means that at ten-thirty Tom and I begin a little poker game in the smoking room. With a number of other people. But after about an hour—around eleven-thirty—I will stand up, stretch, and rub my left eye. That's the signal. One of you will be watching from outside on the deck. You will take turns watching, spelling each other every few minutes so you won't be too noticeable.

"Meanwhile, Tom and I will have properly conditioned the people at the poker table. When you see my signal, you will immediately phone Merrilee here in the suite, and she will come up to the smoking room and walk in quietly to our table and stand there, saying nothing, but looking at everyone around the table solemnly. She will, in effect, be someone who has returned from the dead."

"You mean it?" Merrilee asked.

"You will have risen from the sea, as far as anyone knows. Because everyone thinks you went overboard. That's the effect we want. You're an actress. Act it."

She shivered. "All right. I'll rise dead from the sea."

"As a matter of fact, you could even wet your hair a little. And sprinkle a little water in your face. That's all. We have a lot to do. Let's go."

"I like this," said Betsy. "I'm going to reconnoiter right now, and spot a good window and a phone. Not that I know what I'm doing."

"It's just as well you don't."

Betsy left. Twit-Twit was watching me.

"How many players will we have?" said Tom.

"Better figure on both seven and eight. How are you at dealing from the bottom of the deck?"

"I'd rather do it the way you first suggested. That way we can be sure."

"Okay. Gamble on it. The whole thing is a gamble. If we wind up with six or nine players, you can duck out to the men's room and reshuffle."

"Right." He went into his room to lay out the decks on the bed.

From outside came the crash of a door. The Steak-Lovers were back from dinner. "Do anything you damned well please," he was snarling when the door slammed. Then it slammed again, and I heard him stalk down the hall.

"What are you planning to do?" Twit-Twit said.

"Solve two murders. In fact, I think I already have. Now what remains to be done is to get a confession."

"Sounds dangerous."

"I don't think it will be. But it's the only way I can figure to get the reaction we need."

From the hall came yet another slam from next door. I listened to a woman's heels punch the hall carpet as she moved quickly past, and then I opened our door a crack. Mrs. Steak-Lover was walking with angry quickness down the hall. Behind her, the door of their room was slightly ajar.

I whispered to Twit-Twit. "Do me a favor. Follow that dame and see what she's up to. I'm going into their stateroom a moment. If she acts like she's coming back right away, duck back and warn me. Get going."

She didn't pause to ask questions; she hurried down the hall. I fixed our door latch so I could get back in. No one was in sight. I went next door, stepped inside, and closed the door behind me.

The stateroom was in considerable disarray. Cosmetics were scattered on a dressing table, men's and women's shoes littered the floor, pants both male and female were draped on chairs, and the night stand next to one bed held a bourbon bottle and a used glass. A coffee table in front of the small sofa bore an open case of artists' materials, carefully cleaned brushes, a full complement of casein paints, and a small canvas portraying an ogreish man's face done in nauseating purples and ochres and signed, "Gladys."

I went into the bathroom. There were two more bourbon bottles on the back of the toilet and some letters, suggesting where Steak-Lover did his reading. But the thing that caught my eye was a note, scrawled in lipstick, and stuck to the mirror over the wash basin. It read:

> You will never make me do that again for you, you vile son of
> a bitch

I wondered what 'that' was, although I could guess. I glanced at the letters. They indicated that Steak-Lover's name was Johnson, that he was a radio engineer for a broad-casting company in the Midwest, and that he had left undone something in connection with a studio hookup that he was supposed to have done before he left. "Give my best to your charming Gladys," one letter concluded.

Suddenly I hated Steak-Lover, in a nasty, vindictive way. Perhaps it was the tension I had been under. Perhaps I am just a petty person.

Anyway, there was a pair of gaudy pajamas hanging on the bathroom door and, using his razor which lay on the wash stand, I carefully razored the legs almost completely from the seat, so they would fall apart when he put them on. I thought of the shoes in the other room. I neatly cut almost through all his shoelaces, so they would break when he pulled them tight.

I began to feel better. That is what frustration does; it turns men into beasts. And being a beast can be fun.

A motion at the door to the hall caught my eye. Someone was standing in it—Twit-Twit.

"Having fun?"

"You scared hell out of me. She coming?"

"No. She won't be for quite a while, if I'm any judge."

"Then stand there and watch out for her. I have a few more things to do."

I'd seen some thumbtacks in the paint box. I took them, as well as hairpins from the dressing table, and spread them between the sheets in Steak-Lover's bed. Into his bourbon bottle I poured a quantity of his antidandruff hair tonic.

Some suits and shirts hung in the closet. The vital button on a man's shirt is the one that holds the collar together. With the razor blade I severed the threads of all of Steak-Lover's vital shirt buttons to the point of near-breaking. With the handle of a paintbrush I pushed the toothpaste down into his toothpaste tube and squeezed shaving cream in.

"That'll teach him not to brush after every meal," I said.

Twit-Twit was alternately glancing down the hall and watching what I was doing with fascinated approval. She said, "Don't overlook the bureau."

"Right."

In the bureau drawer there were several pairs of socks; I razored the toes from each and flushed the cut-off toes down the toilet so that he could not make his wife repair them. Spying his toothbrush, I dipped it in a bottle of underarm deodorant. His bottle of bay-rum after-shave lotion I emptied and refilled with bourbon, while Twit-Twit's face filled with fiendish glee.

Finally I took his several fresh razor blades and, without removing them from their paper jackets, individually rubbed the edges against the mirror to dull them.

I looked around. It seemed I had done everything I could to make his world brighter. No matter what else happened, this day would not have been lived in vain.

One last inspiration occurred. I unscrewed half a dozen light bulbs from the wall fixtures and lamps, and tucked them between the mattress and springs of his bed, so when he lay down on it later he would be lulled to sleep by a pleasant series of artillery-like explosions.

I toweled off the objects on which I might have left fingerprints and asked Twit-Twit, "Where'd the wife go?"

"I thought you would never ask. She went for a walk. On the sun deck."

"In this storm? She'll get soaked and freeze to death."

"I don't think so. I followed her up. She met that funny little man who always wears white-mesh gloves. When I last peeked, they were striding the deck in rain and wind. His arm was very much about her. And her head was on his shoulder."

Good for her. She was getting a little of her own out of life, in spite of her husband. I threw the towel on his pillow.

But the mention of her made me think of something else. Would he blame her for my undergraduate jokes?

I dipped a brush in the inkwell on the desk and printed on a sheet of the ship's letter paper:

THE MONSTER WAS HERE

(SIGNED) THE MONSTER

I left it on a chair seat, in view of the door, and we got out and into our suite fast and without trouble.

"Now for the action," I said.

CHAPTER 23

The Other Corpse

At 11:30 we had been playing poker exactly an hour, and I was a few dollars ahead, to my surprise. I had not been playing to win. Mesh-Gloves said, "We should have champagne."

He did not ask if anyone wanted it or preferred something else. He summoned the steward, ordered two bottles of '59 and seven glasses.

Cotton-Hair Pennypacker picked up his hand, looked at it, put it down, and said, "Well, in spite of everything, and that includes the weather, this has been a pleasant voyage."

"I think it has been dull," said Mesh-Gloves.

"Even with that girlfriend of yours?" said Steak-Lover. He didn't quite smack his lips. "She's cute."

"You like her?" Mesh-Gloves asked.

"She's a beautiful girl," said Steak-Lover fervently.

"She bores me. Would you like her tonight? I will send her to you."

There was a little silence after that.

Tom said, "Why don't you bet her in place of twenty blue chips?" and the tension was broken.

But only momentarily, as far as I was concerned. What was going to happen in the next ten minutes was chancy, and could fail horribly. Meanwhile, we bet our hands, and I won a small pot with a pair of kings.

The first officer came into the smoking room, looked around anxiously, and then strolled carelessly toward our table. He leaned over my shoulder and whispered.

"The money was delivered. The man's gloves, they shone. And there were little spots, also red. Of blood, the doctor thinks."

"*Merci*," I said aloud. "I will see the purser the first thing in the morning."

He moved away from our table, but not very far, and pretended to watch the play at another table which was embroiled in *chemin de fer*.

Giorgione said, "Open for a dollar."

Everybody met Giorgione's opening bet. While I waited to draw to a four-card spade flush, I said, "The thing that has disturbed me on this trip is the disappearance of Miss Moore."

"I think it has disturbed everybody," said Cotton-Hair. "Very, very much. Such a lovely girl."

I looked around the table. Steak-Lover, swaying slightly (he must have been on his fifth whiskey), had been joined in his position as official kibitzer by the tall Indian, who was overseeing every hand that he could inspect.

"I got to know her a bit," I said. "So I feel more than a little sorry for her."

"You think she actually went over the side?" asked Widow's-Peak. "I fold."

I folded also. "I don't think there's any doubt, since the ship has been thoroughly searched twice. But more than that, she had considerable reason for killing herself. She was a very haunted person."

"Haunted?" That was Giorgione.

Tom laid down three sevens, and scooped up a fair pot.

"Her mother had told her that she would drown if she ever tried to cross the ocean," I said, "and Merrilee believed that her mother had extrasensory perception."

Giorgione was dealing. "Stud, nothing wild."

I picked up my hand, saw a king, and said, "Open for a dollar."

Steak-Lover was leaning over my chair. "You must be nutty," he said.

I had never seen Cotton-Hair angry before. "If you're going to watch the game, Mr. Johnson," he snapped, "you'll have to eliminate all comment."

We played the hand out, and I drew nothing. Widow's-Peak won with a pair of tens. Then I caught Tom's eye, flexed my shoulders, and rubbed my left eye. That was our signal.

Tom was dealer. As he scooped up the cards, he dropped one, and had to bend down under the table to pick it up; and when he came up again I knew the decks had been switched.

"Five-card draw, deuces wild," he said, and distributed the cards. It was a little hard not to grin at the hand he dealt me. It was a full house, sevens on treys. Giorgione opened, and I wondered what Tom had given him. Everybody stayed except Widow's-Peak. Everyone took three cards except myself and Cotton-Hair, who took only one, as I knew he would. Giorgione checked, and Cotton-Hair bet five dollars. Mesh-Gloves bumped him five, and so did I. Tom and Giorgione both went along and Cotton-Hair said, "Up twenty." Mesh-Gloves folded, and I said, "Up another twenty." Tom looked unhappy but threw in eight blue chips and said, "I'm game—for the time being."

Cotton-Hair looked at me and said, "I'll see you, but that's all."

I laid down my hand. "Full house."

"Wins," said Cotton-Hair. "But just look at this, gentlemen. I almost made history."

He laid down his hand, which consisted, as I knew it would, of a four-card royal flush in hearts, with only the queen of clubs replacing the queen of hearts. Mesh-Gloves made a whistling sound of sympathy. "And it's really only a straight," he said.

"Right, but how close," said Cotton-Hair. "I'm sure I'll never come that close again in my lifetime!"

I looked at Tom. "Where is the queen of hearts?" I asked.

"That's a good question," said Tom. "Where is she?" He looked through the remainder of the deck and said, "She's not here."

"Where's the queen of hearts?" I asked again. "Who has her?"

No one replied, but Cotton-Hair began sorting through the discards. There was no queen of hearts.

"What happened to the queen of hearts?" Giorgione demanded.

"What the hell kind of a deck is that?" said Steak-Lover. "There's no queen of hearts?"

I said, "It's almost symbolic, isn't it? The queen of hearts is missing, and the queen of a great many movie-goers' hearts is also missing."

The table became quiet.

I saw Betsy's nose pressed white against the window across the room. I got up, stretched, and rubbed my left eye. Then I talked fast.

"Wasn't it odd that Mr. Pennypacker should come so close to a royal flush by not drawing the queen of hearts, when the queen of hearts is missing from the deck, and also a girl who is the queen of hearts in another way also has vanished from the deck of the ship? What I really mean is—" I was rattling on, saying anything to hold their attention for ten seconds.

Where *was* she? Tom looked nervous. I suppose that I did, too. Betsy was gone from the window.

I had to keep the talk going. "Another thing that is a puzzle. That hand was a real puzzle."

"It was a kind of Rorschach test," said Cotton-Hair. "I had a four-card royal flush from the start, and needed the queen of hearts. Instead, I drew the queen of clubs."

"Rorschach test is right," I said. "How long have you been teaching psychology, anyway?"

"I got my doctorate at thirty-one," he said. "Thirty-three years ago last June."

Then he looked at me, and saw I was looking at him. Something happened inside of him.

"But what the hell became of the queen of hearts?" Steak-Lover demanded.

By then it did not matter.

Merrilee had come through the far door, and was walking to our table. As people caught sight of her, they stared, and I still have the memory of some woman uttering a shrill scream. I can't blame her.

I had told Merrilee merely to wet her hair and come to our table. The idea had been that she would seem to be a visitation from a watery grave. But I hadn't taken sufficiently into account that she was an actress.

Now she was playing it to the hilt. Her evening dress was dripping wet. Her face and bare arms were festooned with green seaweed. She walked toward us without seeing anything, like an eyeless ghost. Her face was paper-white.

It was so startling that for a second I forgot the lines I had assigned us. Then I leaped to my feet, and said, "Holy Christ, she's come back from the dead."

Tom cried out, "It's her ghost!"

She came slowly to the poker table, looking at everyone around it. She said nothing. I had time for only a glimpse of Cotton-Hair Pennypacker's face, but it was enough. It said everything—except one thing.

He leaped to his feet, hissed words that sounded like, "This is insane!" and reached inside his jacket. He pulled out a thin, blue-steel automatic. He pointed it first at Merrilee and then fanned it around the table.

No one moved. The gun looked efficient.

"You can take us with you, if you want to," I said. "But you can't escape. You can't."

We stared at each other.

"You won't take all of us," said Tom. "That gun doesn't hold that many bullets."

"And besides," I said, "the safety catch is on."

Pennypacker looked down at the gun, and I cannot tell you whether the ship lurched first, or whether I upset the table against him first and then was helped by the rolling sea. But the single gunshot went into the ceiling (I had not seen any safety catch), and he fell over on his back with the heavy table on top of him, and I grabbed the pistol while Tom grabbed his throat.

"There's the murderer," I told the first officer. "You'd better search him. He may have something else on him besides that gun."

Everyone in the room was on his feet, except Pennypacker. Merrilee was looking dazed. Betsy and Twit-Twit were beside her. The first officer and two solemn stewards got Pennypacker up and led him out. He was laughing to himself, his white head rolling.

I breathed deeply.

"For the love of God, take that make-up off," I told Merrilee. "You even scared me—how did you get the seaweed?"

"That's watercress," said Betsy. "From the kitchen."

"That was my idea," said Twit-Twit. "Not bad, eh?"

"And the wet dress?"

Merrilee smiled a chalk-faced smile. "After all, I spent two years at the Actors Studio."

CHAPTER 24

An Injured Knee

"It was a unique problem," I said, "because we knew so much from the start and yet ran into a steel wall as soon as we tried to learn more."

The four of us, plus Merrilee and Widow's-Peak Pennypacker, were sitting in the suite sipping coffee—laced, in some cases, with brandy.

"We knew who was behind all this—Roger Kane—and what he wanted. The real problem was, who was the human apparatus aboard ship that Kane was using to accomplish his purpose?

"The first clue came early, though it wasn't immediately recognizable—the cablegram Richie, or Cotton-Hair, Pennypacker received at lunch the day we sailed. It mentioned a certain Beth and a child weighing seven pounds, eight ounces. At about the same time, this Mr. Pennypacker here received a cablegram saying Boeing stock would go to 78. Merrilee was in suite B-78.

"Either cable might be innocent and genuine, and simply a coincidence. But two of them together simply couldn't be. They clearly were code messages, signed by different faked names, but containing the same information. And that in turn had further implications. Both Pennypackers were working on the same project. Both were getting instructions from New York. But at least one of them did not know of the other's participation, or else a single cablegram to one would have been sufficient for both.

"Once a cable from my office had identified the correct Reginald Pennypacker, a glance at *Who's Who* revealed no Richard Pennypacker, professor of business administration at Grinnell, but did describe a retired West Coast professor of psychology with that name. And his special subjects—like sadism and contrived deception—were highly suggestive.

"I began to sense the curious Tinker-to-Evers-to-Chance nature of the conspiracy. Kane wanted to frighten Merrilee out of making this picture, and he knew of her fears and belief in ESP. What better way than to hire a psychologist versed in cruelty and deception—and calloused to them through long study? Such a man would need physical assistance for some parts of the job. Who better at it than the nation's foremost industrial-espionage agent? And the two cablegrams tied them together.

"Other material clues emerged. *Who's Who* indicated that psychologist Richard Pennypacker had no children. If 'Beth' and the seven-pound, eight-ounce child were code, they tended to confirm the identification. Further, he got mixed up on how many grandchildren he had, saying six at first and then changing it to five in a later conversation. That is not the kind of thing grandparents make a mistake about. Again, he claimed to be a professor of business administration, but he did not know what a 'straddle' is when, as a test, I asked him. And he always wanted to be friendly with us, a good way to allay suspicion.

"This, in fact, was a psychologist's plot, designed primarily to create terror and panic. Murder, incredible as it seems, was only incidental to it. Thus, when Sam Jones refused a bribe to help somehow in the plot, he had to be eliminated. But his murder was turned, with the help of some green make-up and a little stage-dressing, into a powerful convincer to Merrilee that she indeed has precognitive powers. The faked baseball score had the same purpose, and so would the candlelit photograph, had she seen it. Nothing was too outlandish, because only Merrilee presumably could interpret the real meaning of these phenomena.

"In the same vein was the actual, real-life coincidence of the two names, Reginald and Richard Pennypacker. Richard, as brains of the plot, capitalized on this by not changing either—a psychologist's clever trick. For, if two men are hired to work independently on a nefarious enterprise, who would expect them to risk identification by bearing the same name? Richard did adopt a disguise of sorts, of course, by changing his college and academic subject. Reginald here was to be the fall guy, if necessary, as shown by the green-painted rope that was planted in his cabin."

Pennypacker snorted angrily. "Right. When I was hired in New York, this was to be just a surveillance and bugging job. I was to plant a limited-area transmitter in the maid's bed, using a key to be supplied to me—it subsequently came in an envelope, taped to my cabin door—and then await further orders. I had no idea that the operation was being masterminded by someone else aboard ship. It was not until the murder of the maid that I realized what was happening."

"Then you got out fast."

"Right. I purposely made a loud complaint about the green rope and also the meat sheer, to publicly disassociate myself from them, then cabled my resignation. Killing is something I don't mix in."

I nodded. "That little thrust at me with the slicing machine was one more effort at psychological warfare, incidentally. The phone call was made by

Pennypacker's wife, I'm sure. Her cable tonight indicates she was in on the plot.

"And so was Klára, of course—deeply. She had sold some of Merrilee's most intimate secrets to get more money for her own retirement. Who else could know about her dream of the man with the green face? Who knew of the baseball score prediction? I told no one of it. The kindest thing we can say for Klára is that perhaps she believed in the prophecy of Merrilee's mother, and so thought that by betraying Merrilee she was really protecting her from death.

"In any case, Klára was working directly with Richard Pennypacker— the location of the bug proves that. So does the place where Jones's body was originally found. Jones could not have been brought in, alive or dead, hung up, and painted as he was without disturbing a woman sleeping nearby. Why Klára's elimination became necessary we don't know, but a fairly safe guess is that she finally rebelled against something Pennypacker demanded of her, and so sealed her own fate."

I paused to sip coffee.

"But how did you know for sure it was Richard Pennypacker and no one else?" asked Betsy.

"The key question. I learned from a handful of aspirin tablets. As you may know, aspirin fluoresces in ultraviolet light. The person behind all these little and big plots had promised to deliver five hundred francs to the ship's printer, and there was a good chance he would, personally. So I powdered the printer's mailbox with aspirin dust and then arranged with the first officer to have Richie Pennypacker's room searched and all the gloves in it—he'd use gloves, of course, for fingerprint reasons—examined under a UV light. This is a common technique for the nabbing of cashbox filchers, although the professional policeman uses a special fluorescent powder.

"Well, it worked. The first officer signaled me during the poker game what the results of the examination had been. That was the final confirmation.

"As for the game itself—Pennypacker had carefully constructed an atmosphere of terror to accomplish his purpose, and it occurred to me such an operator might himself be especially vulnerable to the same sort of attack. He had reason to think he had driven Merrilee to suicide, so Tom and I worked out some pat hands which would enable me to make remarks about vanished queens that might stimulate his hopes and uncertainties.

"After the stage was set conversationally, I arranged for Merrilee to reappear from the dead. It worked, and made his earlier slip in admitting he was a psychologist quite anti-climactic."

* * * *

There was a short silence.

"What I don't like about all this," said Betsy, "is that this man Kane really caused the whole thing, and yet seems to be so remotely connected with it he'll never be punished."

"Don't be silly." I looked at Pennypacker. "I'm sure he has good lawyers, but I'm also sure that he is not untraceable."

"You're right," said Pennypacker.

"Furthermore, I think Richie will open up when he realizes the murder case against him. And his wife is likely to, also. The cable she sent tonight shows she knew what was going on, though I doubt, with that limp, she took an active part in the physical violence. She could have monitored the bug, and so on, though."

From the stateroom next to us, so loud that it came through the wall, we heard a man roar.

"What the hell happened to my pajamas?"

Twit-Twit and I grinned at each other.

There was a knock at the door, and Tom opened it to admit a page holding a tray with a cable.

"*M'sieu* Pennypackair?" he asked. Widow's-Peak took the cable.

He read it, laughed shortly, and handed it to me.

UNDERSTAND CONGRATULATIONS IN ORDER STOP
REPORT ON LONDON ARRIVAL

His brow furrowed under his widow's-peak. "All I want is out," he said. "If I can help trace some of this back to Kane, I'll be glad to. Okay?"

I said, "Okay." He bowed goodnight and left.

"I've got to go, too," said Merrilee.

Tom and Betsy looked at each other. "I never knew you were so clever with cards," she said. "Next time we go on a trip, it'll be to Vegas, Leftie. 'Night, everybody."

Twit-Twit said, "Merrilee, would you like me to stay with you tonight?" It was nice of her.

"No, but thanks. I feel safe now."

"Well, Deac will take you to your door." And to me, "I'll be waiting."

It wasn't a threat; it was a promise.

As we stepped out into the corridor, we heard a barrage of glassy explosions and strong curses. Steak-Lover had lain down on his bed of light bulbs and thumbtacks.

"You took a lot of chances for me," said Merrilee. Her hand found mine. "You could have been killed."

"It was really the ocean that came to your rescue. It tipped the table over at exactly the right time. So you see, you have nothing to fear from it."

"I think you did the tipping."

Some people came by, saw us hand-in-hand, and looked twice.

While I opened her door for her, she said, "The only trouble is, you don't believe that I am an ESP person. Nobody does."

"Of course I do." But I guess I smiled a little.

She stepped inside. I wanted to get back to Twit-Twit.

"You don't. But if I'm not, then how do I know that when you were about fourteen years old you hurt your right knee playing football? And had to have it strapped up in some sort of sticky tape for weeks? And that it still bothers you at times? I don't know how I know that, but I do."

She was pouting. But I wasn't smiling any longer.

I can still feel the aching of that knee, and the burning pain when the doctor yanked off the adhesive tape....